Song Of The Red Wolf

The Song of The Red Wolf is full of breathless surprises that take you into chaos and mayhem, deep into Tribal Indian territory and century's old murder and vendetta's. It will keep on the edge of your seat. *~ PW Author*

...." House does an admirable job of setting the scene in rural Alabama, and Southern colloquialisms abound, in phrases such as "hot and humid as a toad's back," an apt description for the Southern summer weather....

.... The Franks are certainly likable characters, and the appearances of Chief Running Blood are scary and truly creepy." *~ Kirkus Reviews*

"Fun-loving characters and unexpected events make this story a must-read. The sequels are bound to be as enticing." ~ Deanna Noga

"Definitely a unique and intriguing story, filled with

unexpected twists and turns it will keep you turning the pages. With characters you are sure to relate to and love. The sequels are bound to be as exciting and scary as book one."
~ Columbia Review

"As Entertaining a ghost story whether it's true or not as you are likely to read." - Decatur Review

"Characters you will fall in love with, evil ghost you are sure to hate all with true Southern Charm." - HBReviews

Gathering Storm

Gathering Storm, it's a fun, fast paced book. You will not put it down once you've started reading it. Full of real family drama, a smart and humorous founder of a global Real Estate empire. Henry Enterprises. And the story wouldn't be complete without the conniving and wicked daughter-n-law. Can't wait for book 2. ~ Ladies Book Club, Decatur Chapter

Gathering Storm, it's gets your heart pumping, real stuff happening to real people. Everyone can relate to someone or something that has happened in the story. ~ HB Reviews.

Gathering Storm, a story and characters you can relate to. And my favorite character is Mac. A must read. ~ John Littleton.

Gathering Storm, A winner… A page turner. Full of scandal and lies. With love woven in. Jenna Whitley.

Senses Beyond

Senses Beyond "A faced paced short story that never lets you relax as you read. You won't put it down until you get to the end." ~ *Columbia Review*

Senses Beyond "An ending you won't see coming. Fun and loving characters." ~ *Eva Phillips*

Senses Beyond "I loved the short story, I couldn't put it down. Make sure you read book 1 Song Of The Red Wolf, The Tala Chronicles before you read this book. Can't wait for book 2 of the main series and book 2 of the mini-series." ~ Eloise S.

Senses Beyond "An amazing story of courage, against bullying and danger, it will keep you on the edge of your seat. Read *The Song Of The Red Wolf*." ~ *HB Reviews*

Gathering Storm

The Halcyon Saga

BOOK 1

TONI HOUSE

Source Books© USA

BOOKS BY TONI HOUSE

THE HALCYON SAGA

Gathering Storm Book 1

Web Of Lies Book 2 out *June 2016*

TUSCUMBIA COVE

Butterfly Wings: Book 1 A Spring Harbor Novel: Out June 2016

THE TALA CHRONICLES

Song Of The Red Wolf

1675 Deer Run Ridge: Out Summer 2016

Red Moon Rising: Out January 2017

Winter Snow: Out Summer 2017

The Tala Chronicles: miniseries

Senses Beyond eBook only

Before Tomorrow: Out Summer 2016

Gathering Storm

The Halcyon Saga

BOOK 1

TONI HOUSE

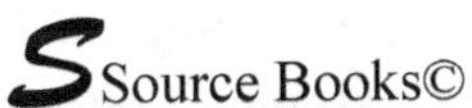

Source Books©

A DIVISON OF SYMSYF PUBLISHING LLC©USA
MAY2016

First Published by *S*Source Books© SYMSYF Publishing,

LLC© USA, May 2016 Copyright © 2016 by "Gathering

Storm" Book 1 of

"The Halcyon Saga"
*S*Source Books© SYMSYF and Toni House

The Cataloging-in-Publication Data is on file at Library of
Congress.

LCCN: 2016905492

Kindle ISBN: 978-0-9961617-6-3

Amazon ISBN: 978-0-9961617-7-0

Ingram ISBN: 978-0-9961617-5-6

Ingram eBook ISBN: 978-0-9961617-4-9

Book design by Jennifer McGuire

Book Interior design by Jennifer McGuire

Book Cover design by Jennifer McGuire

www.ToniHouseAuthor.com

Printed in the United States of America

Distribution: Print and E-Book Amazon, Barns & Noble and where all books are sold.
Please send your comments to
MarketingSourceBooks@gmail.com

*S*Source Books©, Edition 2016 10 9 8 7 6 5 4 3 2 1

Acknowledgements

Thanks to my family and to all my readers, without you I could not do what I love do write and bring you stories that you enjoy.

Chapter 1

Mac Henry sat at his dining room table, waiting for breakfast to begin. If there was one thing he insisted on, it was an early breakfast with his family. His family, meanwhile, knew it was important to maintain a routine. The doctors said it helped his brain make sense of things if there was a schedule he could wrap his day around.

He held his cane in one hand, tip against the floor, hand curled over the lion's head handle. Silver. Heavy. Not a soul living or working at Halcyon Manor had escaped the threat of that cane, either across their backside or against their head.

His stern, straight figure at the head of the long mahogany table was one people expected to see when they visited Halcyon. Never had another man sat at the head of the table since it was built, because Mac Henry had built the home and the company, which funded it from the ground up. He'd started off as an office boy in a real estate office when he was sixteen, having dropped out of school to help support his family after his daddy died. Sixty years later, Henry Enterprises was a real estate empire second-to-none, worth over forty billion dollars. All built with the sweat of his two hands.

Those hands shook somewhat, nowadays. He looked at them, now, as they trembled. There was a time when he could focus hard, concentrate, and get them to stop. It didn't work anymore.

Sometimes he concentrated for so long he'd forget what he was concentrating on. Then he'd take a nap, usually.

He knew he'd be dead soon. Or so senile he'd forget who he was, which was as good as being dead. He couldn't even think about wetting his pants, or being unable to feed himself. He already had the occasional overnight accident, which his housekeeper was sworn never to speak of for fear of death via bludgeoning with a lion's head cane. It was only a matter of time before things went completely downhill.

He looked around at the grandeur he'd created. At least, he'd live out his last days here. Most men had to work up to the day they died, or they barely scraped by on social security or a pension that could just as easily dry up. Not him. He'd worked like the devil all his life, and that work had served him well. His family, too. Even though they didn't have the manners to make it to breakfast on time.

Chapter 2

Just then, a breath of fresh air bounded into the room.
"Good morning, Grandpa Mac!" Maddie, the light of his
life. She bent down, kissed his cheek, gave him a squeeze.
She sat at his left, always, as her mother would have done.

"How are you feeling this morning, Grandpa?" Maddie
smiled at Teresa, who brought out fresh juice and coffee.

"Quite well, considering. Just what do you think you're
doing drinking coffee, young lady?"

She giggled, the dimples showing in her cheeks. "Grandpa,
I'm almost eighteen years old. Lots of kids my age drink

coffee.”

“Coffee stunts the growth.”

“I think I’ve done all the growing I’m gonna do, don’t you?” She winked. He couldn’t help smiling—it was hard to chastise her. “Besides,” she added, “this is nothing compared to some of the things my friends drink. Ooh!” She rolled her eyes comically, always trying to pick up his spirits.

“They were doin’ things like that in my day, too, you know. You young people didn’t invent the trouble you get into.”

“Really?” She leaned an elbow on the table, chin in her hand. “Tell me more.”

“Well, there was this one time. A bunch of friends and I went down to what we called the ‘red light district.’ They were taking me there for my birthday, to meet this woman named Big Reba, and…”

“Mac, I don’t think stories like that are appropriate for a

girl Maddie's age." Maddie's father strode into the room, a frown on his face.

"Oh, Daddy! I'm not a little kid anymore. I know what a whore is." "Madaline!" JT shook his head in disapproval while Mac let out a hearty laugh. "She'll find out, one way or the other, JT," Mac chuckled.

"Yes, well, I don't think today's the day. Especially not at the breakfast table." Mac could see JT barely holding back a smile.

As the maid brought JT his coffee, Maddie cleared her throat. "Daddy, Suzie and I were thinking about going into town today, to do a little shopping for our dorms."

"How much do you need, honey?"

"I don't know. Can I just have your card for the day? You know I have no idea how much these things cost."

"All right, as long as you give it right back when I see you at dinner." JT pulled out his wallet, handing a platinum card across the table to his daughter. Mac watched carefully, noting the sly smile his granddaughter tried hard to hide. He knew the rest of the family thought he was too senile to pick up on their doings, but not a thing escaped his eye.

JT didn't notice, already reading the financial reports. Mac held his tongue. Had it been anyone else in the family, he'd have spoken up, but Maddie had stolen his heart the moment she wrapped her tiny hand around his index finger.

"Where is that wife of yours? And her sons?" Mac demanded, his stomach rumbling.

"Mac, you remember. The boys are on vacation with some friends of theirs. And they're my sons, too—legally, anyway."

"Hmmph. Vacation. What do those boys do with their lives that they need a vacation?"

JT lowered his paper, sighing. "They've both been real busy at school this year. Cal's been doing really well, finally turning his grades around."

"Good—maybe he'll graduate college sometime this decade. How long's he been a freshman? Three years?"

JT ignored this jab. "And Rory's second-string quarterback next season."

"Second-string," Mac muttered. "That's the best either of them will ever be." JT raised his paper diplomatically. Mac glanced at Maddie, who grinned and winked at him. She shared his low opinion of her stepbrothers.

"So where's Bootylicious, then? So I can get my breakfast?"

"Her name's Rebecca, Mac. Which you well know. Though, I guess we should all be glad you didn't call her that to her face."

"Call me what to my face?" Rebecca Depure Rossi floated into the room, squeezed into a dress that looked as though it was poured over her hourglass figure.

"Bootylicious," Mac replied. He loved watching her face turn red. It wasn't embarrassment. It was resentment. He saw JT cringe from the corner of his eye.

"Now, now, Mr. Henry. I can't help what the Good Lord gave me." She bent to kiss her husband, and then took her seat beside her stepdaughter. "Good morning, Maddie."

"Morning." Maddie felt much the same toward her stepmother as Mac did. They were on the same page in just about every way.

"Now I can eat my darned breakfast." Mac slammed his cane into the floor twice, signaling the delivery of the food.

"Mr. Henry, you're gonna wear that carpet right down to the backing with the way you pound on it." Becca smiled tightly. She touched a hand, lightly, to her head. Mac guessed she had one of her hangovers.

"How's the paper looking there, JT?" Mac helped himself to eggs, toast, and four slices of bacon. One thing that hadn't yet left him was his appetite.

"Now, Grandpa." Maddie smiled as she took two pieces of bacon from his plate.

Chapter 3

"Market's still on the rise. It took long enough. It looks like the properties we cleaned up on will finally start bringing in returns. Good thing. I've had the board on my back for months."

"Tell those idiots to stick it up their rear ends! That was my call!"

"Mac, please." JT's eyes flickered toward Maddie. Mac quieted, resentful. He felt a nudge against his leg under the table. Maddie looked at him from beneath lowered lashes. She was smiling.

JT continued. "Regardless, they'll be glad to see the reports coming out at the end of the week. I know I was."

Rebecca cut in. "Sweetie, maybe this would be a good time for us to get away. Now that you have good news to report to the Board. You've been promising me a trip to Europe for months. We could meet up with the boys, all come home together."

"Europe, eh?" Mac snickered. "I'd expect you to want to lay out on a beach, in some skimpy bikini with half your business hanging out."

"There are beaches in Europe, too, Grandpa Mac." Maddie managed to keep a straight face.

Rebecca smiled sugar-coated venom. "Good job, Maddie. I can see how you earned that A in Geography."

"Yes, I did, but I still haven't managed an A in math yet. But, math is your expertise, right? Becca."

"Enough." JT put down the paper. "Becca, honey, now's not the time. I keep trying to tell you; I can't just pick up and go on a whim."

"What's the point of being the CEO of a billion-dollar company if you can't take a vacation?"

"*Multi*-billion-dollar," Mac interjected. "And I don't see you suffering. If ever a woman lived a life of luxury, it's you. You weren't doing too badly before you married into this family, either."

"I'm only thinking about my husband's health, Mr. Henry. I wouldn't want him to become some senile, doddering old man before his time because he overworked himself."

"I think I'm finished eating here," Maddie said. She stood, brushing back her long, dark hair. That hair and her eyes made her the spitting image of her mother. She leaned down, kissing Mac's forehead. She ran a hand over his silver mane, then looked at his cane. "You're looking as shaggy as your lion."

"What difference does it make?" he asked tartly.

"C'mon, Grandpa. Don't you want to look hot for the

ladies? I know my friend Jenna's grandma has the hots for you." She winked.

"Maddie…" JT warned.

Mac grumbled. "Your father's right, Madaline. Those days are long past." He motioned for her to come closer for a kiss. "Get her number for me," he whispered, kissing her cheek.

Chapter 4

Maddie left the room, and the sunshine left with her. Maybe if he hadn't lost his daughter, Maddie wouldn't mean the world to him the way she did. What did his son-in-law find to take the place of his daughter? The cheap floozy currently sitting two chairs away.

He watched as she picked at her fruit salad. At least it wasn't that strange, *keen-wa* stuff she was always eating. After a beautiful, smart, sweet girl like his Madaline, what was JT doing with this piece of trash? She pretended to have class. She knew the right people. But if there was one thing Mac had learned over the course of his long life, it was that a turd couldn't be polished.

"I've got to go." JT rose from his chair, straightening his tie. He shoved his arms into the sleeves of his suit coat. He reminded Mac so much of himself, years ago. He was proud of his son-in-law, despite his misgivings when Madaline first brought him home. At the time, Mac dismissed it as a high school romance. She was a stubborn girl, though. When Mac asked his daughter to wait until after college to make any decisions on marriage, she agreed. She married Johnathan Thomas Rossi the day after college graduation.

This left Mac alone with Becca. She was careful not to meet his eyes. "You can have one, if you want," he murmured.

"One what?"

"A drink. I know you're dying for one."

She smiled brilliantly. "What gives you that idea?"

"The way your hands are shaking. You tied one on last

night. It happens. The hair of the dog is the best thing for it." He watched as her smile faded.

She stood, glaring at him. "You're an awfully hateful old man," she hissed.

"Finally, her true colors show. I like you so much better when you stop pretending to be a lady. That's not difficult, though, seeing as how intensely I dislike you the rest of the time."

She crossed her arms. "It's a good thing you won't be around for many more years to deal with me." Mac had to laugh to himself as she walked away. She had spirit, at least.

Chapter 5

"JT Rossi's office." JT walked past his assistant's desk, throwing her a wave as he entered his office. Sometimes it felt as though this was the only refuge he had. It was easier to come here and shut the door than sit at the breakfast table some mornings. He'd been in hostile board meetings more pleasant than that.

Pressley buzzed him. "I have Senator Marlowe's office on the line."

JT picked up the handset. "Put him through." Seconds later, a click, then, "Rossi, you disgusting crook. I finally catch you in your office when you're not out robbing elderly widows."

"You should know about robbing the public, you dirty politician." Both men laughed. "What's up, Steve?"

"Not much, man. Been hoping to catch you for the past week or so. I got word of a potential business deal that I think you'd be interested in."

"Really?" JT knew his oldest friend well enough to read his tone of voice. He'd heard it enough times when they were roommates in college, and Stephen had wanted to tell him about the best new place to score weed or girls. He sounded like he had a great secret to share, one not everybody could be privy to. Why? Was the deal not completely on the up-and-up?

Stephen continued, "The information isn't exactly available to the public yet." Yes, there was JT's answer.

He chuckled. "Senator, you sound like you're throwing a favor your friend's way before letting everybody else have a fair shot at it. That's not strictly kosher, is it?"

"Hey—I owe you."

"You don't owe me anything," JT said. "We do favors for each other because we're friends. That's it."

"Then consider it a friendly favor. Maybe you and I can get together for lunch sometime this week to discuss it?"

JT mulled the idea over. If it was worth Stephen giving him a call—and he'd said he'd been trying to get a hold of him for a week—it might be worth hearing him out. JT told himself it was out of friendship.

"Sure. Have your girl call Pressley. We'll get it set up."

"Fantastic. I'll see you then." JT heard the click, knew Stephen had hung up. He sat with the receiver against his chin. He wondered if it was a good idea to get involved with a politician in anything but a personal relationship. They played on a much bigger field than the average businessman. Yes, Henry Enterprises had holdings in nearly every developed country in the world, but that still seemed small compared to the level of player politicians got involved with.

The least he could do was hear the man out. They'd been friends since the first day of Freshman year when they met in their dorm room. Funny how Fate had a way of working things out. He could just as easily have ended up being roommates with some stuck-up jerk. Stephen was anything but. They'd hit it off immediately.

That conversation was enough to take his mind off the unpleasantness at the breakfast table. He dove headfirst into work. Reviewing contracts and checking in on the progress of the quarterly reports for the upcoming meeting with the members of the board. Family was the last thing on his mind by lunch time.

Then, Pressley buzzed in. "Mr. Rossi, I have a Veronica von Halkein on the phone for you?"

"Oh, you've gotta be kidding," he whispered, then picked up the receiver to speak to Pressley directly. "Did you tell her I was here?"

"I said I would check as I usually do. Should I tell her you've left for lunch already?" JT checked the time—was it already that late?

"Uh, yes. Tell her I stepped out to lunch; get a message. Make *sure* she gives you a number."

Veronica. How long had it been? It had to be nearly ten years. She'd come to the wedding, staying in one of the guests houses at Halcyon for four weeks before disappearing. And von Halkein? His private investigator had told him she'd married some sort of Austrian Baron. Maybe it was German.   JT couldn't remember.

He needed time to collect his thoughts before his sister came barreling back into his life. She hadn't spoken a word to him in all these years. She had to want something.

He almost couldn't wait to tell Becca. If there was one person in the world his wife was afraid of, it was Veronica.

Ronnie was a force of nature. She had an intense energy about her, the sort that made men and women crumble in front of her. When she made up her mind about something, there was no question of whether or not she'd get her way. It was just a matter of when.

Yes, telling Becca about this would be fun.

Becca had been a worry for him lately. He didn't often let himself get distracted by personal thoughts while in the office, but there had been an almost unbearable amount of tension between her and Maddie, then between her and Mac. It seemed to be escalating while he stood in the center, wondering what was happening.

He'd known what he was getting into when he had married Becca Depure, hadn't he? He hadn't gone into the wedding with his eyes closed. While he had never been serious about a woman since Madaline died, he'd known plenty casually. There was no way he'd bring a woman into his daughter's life unless he were certain she was in it for the long haul. So when he met Becca, with her honey hair and tinkling laugh and mile-long legs (and her husband's life insurance payout), he knew he was in for a challenge.

Back then, she'd been different. He'd known on some level she was reeling him in. Maybe it was the fact she was already a mother that appealed to him. She seemed to dote on her boys. JT liked the idea of a ready-made family, but he knew there would be growing pains. It was never easy bringing two families together, especially when the kids were eight, ten, and twelve years old as theirs had been.

Maddie had needed a mother. Becca had twelve years of experience. She was also beautiful, exciting, smart, and funny. A pale ghost compared to the woman he'd married when he was twenty- two. But a substantial woman. One he saw himself building a life with.

Now it seemed as though she was always unhappy. He wanted to change that. A lot of her unhappiness had to do with the way hers and Maddie's personalities clashed.

Maddie was so much like her mother that it scared JT sometimes. He and Mac had long talks in JT's home office back when Maddie was younger, and even sometimes after Mac had the stroke. The old man still remembered raising his daughter—or, rather, the way his wife had raised his daughter. He told JT stories that made him laugh while simultaneously making him cringe. Could he expect his own daughter to pull stunts like that?

Becca didn't take well to having her wishes overruled, but try as he might, JT couldn't help deferring to his daughter. Even though he knew he should take his wife's side to present a united front, he had too big a soft spot for those blue-green eyes, the image of her mother's. He knew Mac felt the same way.

It was a recipe for disaster. Take one headstrong little girl, add two men who adore her and give her what she wants, add in a heavy pinch of a similarly headstrong stepmother. Stand back and watch the sparks fly.

When he allowed himself the time, JT worried about how Maddie would end up. What would her future be? He knew she wasn't interested in living the life Becca and so many other wives of rich men lived. She looked down on that lifestyle and the women who lived it. She was going to Cornell. She was an athlete and a serious student. She wanted to build a life for herself.

What happened when her first boss yelled at her? Would she yell back? Would she even be able to keep a job? He sighed, knowing they'd spoiled her far too much.

Regardless, he loved her fire. Her spirit. He admired it, as he did in anyone who possessed it. Madaline. Veronica. Mac.

JT smiled, thinking about his father-in-law. He could have sent JT and Maddie packing once Madaline died. Instead, he'd insisted they live with him. He was all alone, and he still intended to bring JT into the business—regardless of whether his daughter lived. It had been a godsend. He'd never stop feeling grateful.

Look where he now sat, as a result. At the head of the largest real estate empire in the world. Mac had built it, but JT maintained it and watched it grow even further. Where would be he otherwise? A single father, trying to make ends meet?

Perhaps that was why he felt the need to prove himself. Otherwise he'd be just another classic example of a man taking advantage of the family he'd married into. He had too much pride to allow that.

Maddie had that same pride. Who would she become? He'd love to see her be groomed to take over the business once he stepped down. She had the smarts, the inner steel to take the reins and bend others to her will. Maybe that would be her path. She'd never make a good underling. He could just see her sitting in a cubicle, being bombarded with requests to perform mundane, meaningless tasks.

She'd last a day, tops.

She had her own life to live, though. He couldn't force her. He could only do what parents always do: hope for the best while making sure she didn't do anything too stupid.

Chapter 6

Maddie liked to take a walk outside after breakfast, no matter how humid the mornings sometimes got at this time of year. Anything was better than smothering half to death in that house, around the breakfast table.

She loved her father. She adored her grandfather. She detested the woman she refused to think of as a mother, no matter how much her father had encouraged it over the years. There had been no chance. The two of them hated each other, and they always would.

Daddy was so clueless about things. He was good at

business, and he was good at being a father. He loved her. He was never anything but good to her. He even tried to be good to those two goons he adopted, Becca's evil offspring. Rejects, both of them. Daddy did his best.

He just didn't get it. Probably because he was always so busy. He saw things the way he wanted them to be. She'd once heard Granddaddy say that was the way a good businessman should be. He saw his world a certain way, and everybody around him had to fall into line around it. Only not everything fell in line. Daddy didn't see that. He was blind to so much.

Like the way Becca hated her. It didn't bother Maddie one bit, but she knew it would crush him if he understood it was more than just rivalry that stood between them. Maddie had her father's undivided love and attention. There was no mistaking that, so there was no contest.

The problem was the way she saw straight through Becca from the minute they met. She might have only been eight at the time, but Grandpa had always told her she was the best judge of character he'd ever met. She'd always been able to know what people were really after, no matter what they said or how sweetly they said it. She didn't know how she knew. It was something she was born with.

And she knew, in her soul, that her daddy's girlfriend was fake. She smiled. She laughed. She was very pretty. But she was cold inside. Her eyes had been a giveaway. There was nothing in them.

Kids can pick up on things like that. If a person's eyes are cold and empty, kids don't have all the built-up excuses people tell themselves as they get older to fall back on. *She's had a hard life*, or *She just lost her husband.* Children see what they see. Maddie had seen a gold digger and had made sure everybody knew it.

That had set the tone for the next ten years.

She reached the pool, sparkling and inviting in the stifling humidity. She had put on her bathing suit after breakfast, intending to take a dip before continuing her walk, and now stripped off her t-shirt and shorts to reveal a white bikini before diving in.

A few laps back and forth cleared her head a bit. She was

still steaming from the fight she'd had with her father the night before, which he'd carefully avoided mentioning this morning. That was another thing about him. He'd always rather avoid hashing things out.

"Hey, Rossi." Maddie turned from her breaststroke, finding her friend Elix standing by the side of the pool.

"Elix. What are you doing over here? Aren't you usually at the stables at this time of day?"

 "You know I am. I was wondering where you were. Lady's needing a ride. She asked me to come look for you."

Maddie grinned. She rode her favorite filly almost every day; it was exercise for both of them. "It's so hot. I figured I'd take a swim first."

"It's brutal out here." Elix wiped sweat from his brow with the back of his arm. "Jump in!"

"What? Come on."

"I mean it! Nobody's here to see. You work here, Elix. You're not a slave. Nobody's going to care if you cool off real quick. Come on!"

"I don't have a suit on," he pointed out.

"Are you going commando today?" He shook his head. "Then you're all set. Just wear your shorts. I won't watch, if that's what you're worried about. It's awfully cool and comfortable in here." She flashed him another grin.

Seconds later, Elix was pulling off his shirt. Maddie told herself she shouldn't look at him 'that way', but she couldn't help it. He had a gorgeous body. All that physical labor, not to mention the football he used to play, kept him in fantastic shape.

He did a cannonball into the pool, making Maddie squeal when the water splashed her. He surfaced, laughing. "You're right. This feels amazing."

They swam around for a little while, not saying much of anything. She'd always been able to hang out with him like this. They'd been friends for a few years, even though

Elix was twenty-two. The same age as her stepbrother, Cal. The two of them couldn't be less alike if they tried, except for one very important similarity. They'd both gotten into serious trouble in the past.

"So, what's going on with your birthday?" Elix asked, arms crossed over the edge of the pool. His shoulders and back were broad, tanned. Maddie reminded herself to stop staring.

"Ugh, I'm so sick of fighting with them about it." "No party?"

"It looks that way. They're completely ridiculous." Maddie swam to where Elix was resting and joined him. She crossed her arms over the edge, resting her chin there.

"You're the one who had the big kegger when they were out of town." "It wasn't that big."

"Maddie. There were, like, a hundred people there."

"Okay, correction: I didn't *mean* for it to get that big. I only invited a few friends. It got out of hand. That part wasn't my fault."

"They probably wouldn't have cared if kids weren't smoking pot."

Maddie shrugged. "So what? I wasn't the one doing it. That's what should really matter. I've never done it, and I never will. They know me better than that."

"Who turned you in? Your grandfather?"

"Grandpa Mac? Nah. He would never. Shoot, if he'd been awake he might have asked to join us. It was one of the staff. I don't know which one. But something got broken, some vase Daddy really liked. When he asked them about it, they dimed me out. I was *this* close to getting away with it." She held her thumb and forefinger an inch apart. Elix laughed.

"Right. I'm sure you were."

"I was! Anyway, they're the biggest hypocrites. Acting like they were so innocent when they were my age. Parents suck." Elix fell silent, making Maddie feel awful.

His parents had died when he was a little boy. "I'm sorry. I always say stuff without thinking about it first."

"It's okay." He swam away, doing a lap. Maddie watched his lean body glide through the water. She hated seeing somebody like Elix having to work in the stables and around the grounds like some servant. It could have been a lot worse for him, though, after what he did.

When he surfaced, treading water, he asked, "What are you up to today?"

"I was gonna do a little shopping. For school. I got my dad's platinum card." She smiled. "Mmm-hmm. Just for school, huh?"

"You're so suspicious." "I know you."

She shrugged. "Whatever. He never checks his statements. Just has his assistant pay the bill." "I know what you do when you go out. You have lunch at nice places and act like a big shot." "I don't have to act," she said archly.

"Now you sound like your stepmother."

"Watch it." All pretense of joking around vanished from her voice. Elix knew better than to cross the line like that. "I'm nothing like that woman."

Elix shook his head. "Your dad's a nice guy. You should stop taking advantage of him." Maddie frowned, pushing herself up and out of the pool. She didn't need a speech. "Hey, Maddie. I'm sorry. I didn't mean to say…"

"You meant it," she snapped, pulling on her shorts. "You can't take it back now."

He got out of the pool, confronting her. "You're right. I meant it. And now you're going to run away like a baby because nobody can tell you anything you don't want to hear. Right?"

"Yes, Elix. You know me *so* well." She rolled her eyes, pulling her tee over her long, wet hair. It immediately soaked through the thin cotton.

"Better than you think. And you don't like it."

"I just don't like *you*." With that, she turned and stalked off. She got the last word in, at least.

Screw him. She walked away, stomping her feet. He had a lot of room to talk, after the stunt he pulled. He wouldn't need to work at Halcyon if it hadn't screwed up so badly. He could have graduated college this year. Maybe he could have been drafted into the NFL—he was that good. No. Instead, he mucked stables and pulled weeds. Her father's pity, and the closeness of Elix's family with the Henrys, were the only things keeping Elix out of jail. He was so quick to pass judgment on her.

So what if she liked to shop? It was all she had to occupy her time right now. No school, no job. Daddy had wanted her to intern somewhere over the summer, but she hated the idea. She'd turned on the charm, telling him she needed just one more summer to hang out and have fun before going off to college and becoming a woman. She wanted to spend as much time as possible here at home before she had to leave. That had done it. It never took long to get him to see things her way.

And now here was Elix with his corny judgments. She should have slapped his face. Maybe it would have reminded him who worked for whose father.

She went back to the house, running up the wide staircase and down the hall to her room. She punched a pillow and threw it to the floor, then kicked it. Who did he think he was, telling her how to act?

Maddie sat on the bed, out of breath from her temper tantrum. Wasn't she too old for things like this? Even she saw how childish she was acting, now that the hot flash of anger had passed. She didn't like people telling her what to do or who to be. It was something she knew needed working on if she ever planned to live as an adult. She wouldn't be a professional trophy wife like her stepmother.

She'd have to go down and apologize to Elix later. It was something she was trying to do more often, now that she was out of high school. Owning up to her mistakes. This would be good practice. Maybe she'd buy him a little something while she was out.

After a quick shower to rinse off from the pool, Maddie dried her long hair and picked out a special outfit for lunch. Elix was right, of course. They weren't just going shopping. She and Suzie loved going to the Four Seasons for lunch. It was the place to see and be seen. And they never carded when she asked for a drink, knowing her family. It paid to have a last name people respected.

She chose a cute Marc Jacobs wrap dress and white sandals, using a long scarf as a headband. With her big sunglasses, she'd look chic and elusive. Just what she wanted to be today.

As she was tying the scarf, she caught her own eyes in the mirror. Blue-green, just like her mother's had been. Not that she'd know. She'd never met her mother.

Elix had her thinking about herself again. Was it really so wrong to have a nice lunch and a shopping spree on her father's charge? If she'd asked flat-out to do it, he'd have said yes. What was the big deal, then?

She was lying. That was the problem. Why did she feel like she had to lie?

This was all Elix's fault. Making her think about things

like this. She'd been looking forward to the day, too. Now she was huffy again, grabbing her bag before hurrying down the stairs and out the door, slamming it shut behind her. The Mercedes she'd gotten for her sixteenth birthday was waiting in the turnabout. She gunned the engine, taking off down the long, wide driveway toward the front gates.

As she zipped along, she saw Elix. He was watching, waiting for her to pass. She gave him the finger without glancing his way.

Toni House

Chapter 7

Becca peeled away from the house in her Porsche, on her way to the salon before lunch with the girls.

One of her many vices was fast driving. As far as she was concerned, fast was the only way to go. It was the closest thing to flying. Her, the car, the road.

Her thoughts hadn't been on her driving this morning. That old buzzard hadn't been wrong when he accused her of tying one on the night before. How had he known? She always tried to be discreet when she drank alone. He had eyes in the back of his head, the dirty old man.

How much longer would the old buzzard hang on? When she married JT, the old man was practically on his last legs. That was ten years ago. Was he drinking the blood of virgins? He was the second biggest thorn in her side, and he just wouldn't go away.

She tried to calm down. It wouldn't do to show up at the salon all worked up. There were gossipy old vultures everywhere, waiting for her to show the slightest signs of weakness so they could jump on her. They'd pick the flesh from her carcass and take pleasure in it.

Deep breaths, Becca. Why was she in such a terrible mood today? All this thinking about vultures and buzzards. Their daily family breakfasts certainly didn't start the day off right. If she had her way, breakfast in bed would be the rule. The moment she was free of Mac's silly rules, that would be the first one she changed.

It made no sense, following the whims of a senile old man. What if he decided everyone should run around the house with their underwear outside their clothes? Would JT frown in disappointment if she complained about that, too?

Ten years of seeing that disappointed frown. Why had he married her if she was such a disappointment to him? Oh, right. Because she was pretending to be Good Becca back then. Compliant Becca. Becca who wanted a rich husband whose father-in-law was practically dead. Yet Mac was still here. Life was funny that way.

JT had fallen in love with the best version of her. The version she showed strangers, the version she believed she could be all the time if given the chance. But life was always getting in the way. How could a woman take control of her life the way she needed without being seen as a shrew?

Chapter 8

From the time she was a little girl, Becca had known she was meant to live a life of leisure. She'd grown up watching women who lived that way, the ladies who visited her daddy's gas station in their fabulous cars. Sitting behind the wheel and applying lipstick, while her father filled their gas tanks and washed their windshields. Sometimes they'd be driving, other time their liveried drivers would be sitting behind the wheel while the ladies sat in the back.

Sometimes they would extend a perfectly manicured hand out the window to give her father a tip. Most of the time they wouldn't. "You'd think women with money like that would be a little more generous with it," her mama would grumble.

"That's why they have money like that. They hold onto it for dear life," Daddy would answer. It didn't bother him. He was always easygoing, not caring much about 'the good life'. As long as he had a few extra bucks at the end of the week for a trip to the bar to laugh with his pals, he was happy.

Mama, on the other hand, had different ideas. She'd scrimped and saved to give her only daughter the best of everything. She took in sewing, babysat, and scrubbed floors. Anything it took to give her daughter the little things.

It was never enough. Even the best they could afford was secondhand and looked it. Resentment had taken root inside Becca's heart and grown. She smiled in the faces of the rich girls, whose parents could afford to get them nice, new things, while hating them in her heart. Sometimes it felt like she'd turned to stone in those years. Nothing mattered more to her than enjoying the money her strategic marriages had afforded her.

That and her boys. They would take their place in society as the sons of JT Rossi. They would have everything she couldn't have as a girl. That was why she'd insisted on JT adopting them right after the wedding. It involved making the sacrifice of adopting JT's brat of a daughter, but sacrifices were necessary when the bigger picture was at stake.

The tires squealed when the Porsche came to a stop in front of the salon. She handed the keys to the valet, carrying her Birkin bag over her bent arm as she sailed through the front doors. Just stepping foot inside this pink confection of a place made her feel better. She was handed a mimosa, then directed to a plush chair in which to wait until her stylist was ready.

Shana Mulvaney, social queen, was waiting for her own stylist. "Becca! Darling, you look absolutely anorexic! I *have* to know your secret." The old crone was always looking for the fountain of youth.

Somebody needed to point her in the direction of a wizard,

because she looked every minute of her fifty-five years. *Thirty-five*, if you asked Shana, which was ridiculous.

"Thanks, love. I just did a cleanse over the weekend. I feel fantastic." Becca smiled brilliantly and waved as the older woman was led back to her stylist's chair. She sighed deeply, sipping the mimosa. Mac had been right about the drink. She felt better already.

Chapter 9

Ten years. One year between marriages. Another thirteen with her first husband. She had been living the life she and her mother had dreamed of since she had managed to wrangle Frank Depure at eighteen. She'd laughed behind her hand at the reactions of those same rich girls who had always laughed at her. Frank had been everything she was looking for: rich, indulgent, trusting. With a ten- million-dollar life insurance policy.

Becca wasn't as young as springtime anymore, but she could pass for her early thirties on a good day. She secretly preferred when her boys were out of town or, better yet, out of the country.

Otherwise, people saw the two of them, saw her, and started doing math in their heads.

"Becca, Iris is ready for you." Becca uncrossed her long, slim legs and followed the shampoo girl to Iris's chair. Only Iris knew how much of Becca's honey blonde hair was turning gray. Hence the generous tip the stylist always received.

"What do you have in mind today, Mrs. Rossi?"

"The usual, dear. Touch-up and trim, then a blow-out."

"Do you have anything special planned today?" The stylist draped a cape over Becca's Lilly Pulitzer dress, then began her work.

"Just lunch with my friends. What's new with you, Iris?" Most women liked chatting with their stylist. Becca preferred absorbing the dirty secrets the woman shared. Some idiots treated their visit to the salon like a visit to a confessional. Iris was always happy to share what she heard.

Becca listened, intent as always. Gathering information. Who was cheating on whom? Whose husband was secretly gay? Whose daughter had been spirited off for an abortion under the guise of a European vacation? It was all filed away in her prodigious memory in case she needed ammunition against a rival.

Toni House

Chapter 10

Lunch with the girls went much the same as it always did. Drinks flowed, and nobody ate much of anything.

"Lauralee, how's Evie doing now that the school year is over?" Becca swirled the olive in her martini.

"She's fantastic. Interning this summer with Senator Marlowe. Richard is sending a very nice bottle of whiskey JT's way to thank him for helping set that up."

"What's the good of having a Senator as a friend if you can't use the connection to your advantage?" All four women laughed.

"And how do the boys like their vacation?" Genevieve asked, pushing the leaves of her garden salad around on the plate.

Becca raved. "I am so glad they're getting a chance to see Italy. JT and I went there on our honeymoon, of course, and I've wanted so much for them to go. Now's the time, after all. Before family and responsibilities call."

"It's a wonder you never got back there after all this time," Carly pointed out. She was constantly bragging about the trips her husband took her on.

"I've always envied your ability just to pick up and go. I'm sure it's so much easier when there are no children to consider." Becca lifted her martini to her lips, watching childless Carly's smile slip away.

"And how did Cal and Rory do in school this year?" Lauralee asked, changing the subject.

"Excellent. We're so proud of them." Becca beamed, playing the happy mother. In reality, she didn't want to invite any further conversation about the boys. It was another one of the games they played. Everyone knew what a disappointment the boys had been, but none of them would say it. They'd only drop hints.

"Have you decided whether or not there'll be a party for Maddie's eighteenth?" Gen asked. Becca was glad for the change of subject, though she bristled at the mention of her stepdaughter. The other three women chuckled knowingly.

"If Mac had his way, we'd throw a party every day for her. Same thing with JT. They both spoiled the pants off that girl." She emptied her glass, signaled to the waiter for another. "Frankly, I don't think we should be celebrating this child when we caught her friends red-handed, smoking pot and drinking under our roof last month. What do I know? I'm just the wicked stepmother." They hadn't exactly caught her in the act but rather heard about it from the staff after the fact. It was just as bad in her eyes.

"Just be sure to let us know if you decide to throw it. I will just have to see this." Gen winked.

"You'll be there for sure. I'll need a support system." The four laughed again, Becca's laugh masking her irritation.

Chapter 11

Becca excused herself from the table after her second martini, citing a meeting with her lawyer. She knew once the air kisses and promises to get together again faded, the topic of conversation would turn to her. It was the price of having female friends.

She was a little tipsy but nowhere near impaired. She knew JT wouldn't approve of her driving after having lunch with the girls—he'd always insisted she use one of their drivers, but she wasn't Miss Daisy yet.

That conversation about Maddie had her blood boiling. For

ten years, she'd been barely tolerating the little witch.
Even as a girl, when the two of them first met, Becca had
seen right through her. The precociousness, the charm, the
quick wit. Even the freckles that had dusted her nose. All
were like nails on a chalkboard as far as Becca was
concerned.

"You would never know I'm the mistress of this
household!" She'd once hurled this accusation at JT in the
middle of an argument. She'd meant it with every fiber of
her being, too. Maddie called all the shots, came and went
as she pleased, and was the apple of everyone's eye. She
even sat across from her father at the dining room table, a
seat Becca should have filled. Nobody seemed to see the
problem with this.

In her most honest moments, the moments in which she
looked clearly at herself, Becca knew her biggest problem
with Maddie was the uncanny knack her stepdaughter had
for seeing her true motivations. From that memorable first
dinner, when Becca had brought the boys to Halcyon to
meet the family and Maddie had called her a gold digger,
Becca had known the girl would be her greatest

adversary.

Becca was biding her time. She knew there would come a day when she'd unseat the unspoken Queen of Halcyon Manor. Sending Maddie off to school in the fall would be a good first step. She would show up Cal and Rory, of course, but that would be worth it as long as she was out of the house.

Then Becca could take her rightful place at Halcyon after ten long years. Changes would come.

Chapter 12

"Yes, baby…that's it...keep going…"

JT was seated at his desk, looking over some paperwork his assistant had just delivered.

She pushed his chair back and crawled under his desk. And now he was whispering encouragement to her as she un zipped his pants and grabbed hold of him as he sprung free.

He heard her muffled moan as she worked him. She got off on this nearly as much as he did. By the time she finished, she'd be soaking wet. The thought made him throb as her mouth moved up and down his…

"That's right…work it…" He signed off on a set of contracts with a developer, then closed his eyes as Pressley's tongue flicked just beneath the tip where it met the shaft. She stroked his thick shaft as she went.

"Yeah…yeah…faster…" Her hand flew over him, up and down. His eyes were closed, all work forgotten, as she pulled harder on the top.

"Ohhhh…Ohhhh!" He shuddered as he finished.

He rolled away from the desk, allowing his assistant to come out from underneath. She was flushed, breathless.

JT cleared space on his desk, sitting her down. She placed her feet on the arms of the chair, then leaned back on her elbows. He discovered he was right when he hiked up her skirt. She'd soaked through her panties.

"Do you get excited when you take me?" he asked, stroking her with his thumb. She whimpered, grinding her hips.

"Yeah…I love it…" she whispered.

"You must. You're so wet," he said. She moaned, lifting her hips.

"Lick it," she begged. "Please." He slid her panties down, tossing them to the floor before diving between her legs. She barely stifled a loud moan.

"Shh…" he whispered, going back to her wetness. Touching and licking her most private parts. Sliding two fingers into her, pumping in and out in time with his tongue's movements. She went wild, her hips bucking against him. Moments later she shuddered, and trembled with her release.

Chapter 13

The thing about sex in the workplace, JT thought as he and his assistant got themselves put together, *is not being able to relax afterward*. No matter how hot it was, how satisfying, minutes later it was back to business. By the time Pressley opened the door to his office, signed papers under one arm, it was as though nothing had happened.

"Thank you, Pressley," he said as she was leaving.

"Thank you, Mr. Rossi." She sent a wink in his direction before disappearing.

She was incredible. Young and sexy, with a perfect body

and the face of an angel. She was also adventurous, always up for anything he had in mind. JT wondered how much of that had to do with her attraction to him, and how much of it was due to her need for approval. Either way, she made coming to the office more interesting.

He stepped into his private bathroom to freshen up, combing back his thick, dark hair and checking his smooth-shaven cheeks for any traces of lipstick. While washing his hands, he caught his eye in the mirror over the sink. He looked away quickly, suddenly ashamed of himself.

What was he doing? How many men did he know whose lives were irreparably complicated by affairs with their assistants? Unwanted pregnancies, ugly divorces, enormous alimony payments. It was the oldest story in the world, one which Mac had advised him against a long time ago.

"Stay away from inner-office nookie," he'd said, in his usual blunt manner. JT had been so surprised he'd spit Scotch all over himself.

"What made you think I'd be interested in that?" he'd asked, wiping off the front of his shirt and laughing. Back then he'd been naïve, sure such a thing would never appeal to him.

"Because you're a normal, red-blooded man, and nobody could blame you for having your head turned by a short skirt or a flash of cleavage. It happens to all of us, believe me. And it is never, ever worth it in the end. Go to the men's room. Take care of it yourself. Leave it at that."

JT had done his best to listen to Mac's advice, but when a girl walked in who reminded him so much of Madaline it had hurt, he'd hired her on the spot. Christina was the one who ended their affair, moving to another city to marry her long-distance boyfriend. That had been a relief, absolving JT of the burden of breaking things off. She'd been mature about it.

This new girl, Pressley, JT thought might be a different story. She was younger, more impressionable. She seemed a little too involved in their relationship. He was afraid to end it, for fear of how she'd react. And he didn't want to, since she gave the best oral he'd ever gotten. She also reminded him of Madaline. The waterfall of dark hair, the blue eyes.

At first he'd told himself he wouldn't be so tempted to stray from his marriage if his wife hadn't been so hot and cold. One day she'd be all over him, making him feel like the only man who'd ever existed. The next they were virtually strangers. Lately, it had been much more the latter than the former.

The truth was that he'd never gotten over losing his first wife. He'd loved her since he was fifteen, just a stupid high school kid whose only experience with women had come in the form of his stepfather's porn DVDs. Then he'd met Madaline, and the world changed. She was everything to him, from the day the met until she day she died. And for the nearly eighteen years since.

He felt sorry for Becca in his more honest moments. It wasn't her fault she couldn't measure up to a ghost. He did love her, always had, but not the same way he'd loved Madaline when she was alive.

She was special. There was no other way of describing her.

She could have been a world-class pianist or a Michelin-star chef. She was even a good painter and photographer. She'd chosen to marry him, to settle down as his wife, when there were endless opportunities elsewhere. Maybe she should have run off instead of marrying him. She might be alive today. Then again, he wouldn't have Maddie.

He remembered how happy Madaline had been when she found out she was pregnant, only six months into their marriage. She'd wanted to trying for a baby start right away, even though JT wasn't sure they were ready. She'd pointed out they were living in a guest house on Halcyon property, so they had no bills. He was making a good salary, working for her father. There would never be a better time.

JT had wanted to wait until they could move off, start a life of their own. His wife hadn't been so patient. How many times had he wished he'd put his foot down? He could have had her that much longer.

She'd been an avid reader, sometimes spending an entire day curled up in her favorite chair with a book. He'd come home from work to find her exactly where he left her, with the same book in her hands. She would lose time. When she was on bed rest, her reading picked up even more. She would read five, six books in a week.

Not that it mattered. All that knowledge, and all that talent, went with her.

Now he felt doomed to spend the rest of his life chasing after that feeling of being completely enamored with a woman, feeling totally connected to her. The older a person got, the fewer chances there were for such connections. We never love as strongly as we did when we were kids.

His love for Becca had always been a shadow of what he'd felt for Madaline. He'd tried to tell her in every way he knew how that he'd lost part of himself when he lost her. At the time, with Becca being a fairly new widow, he thought she'd be able to relate. As time went on it became clear she didn't love her first husband so much as she was fond of him. There was no comparison.

Who could blame him, then, for looking for ways to fill

the void?

Maybe Maddie hadn't gotten all of her pigheadedness from her mother. He sounded about as childish as his daughter did when she threw a tantrum to get her way. Besides, wasn't 'I had to fill the void' one of the oldest excuses for infidelity? Right up there next to 'we were already emotionally separated for a long time'.

Wasn't he better than that? Didn't he pride himself on doing things differently from other powerful men? He'd worked hard to avoid falling into the traps of wealth. Now here he was, getting back to work after a tryst with his assistant. He was a cliché, after all.

It wouldn't happen again. He'd find a way to break it off with her. Or so he told himself after every encounter they had.

Chapter 14

"I wish I could totally look forward to going away, like you do." Maddie's mood had dropped again. What was with her today? She wasn't PMS'ing.

She and Suzie were sitting in the restaurant at the Four Seasons, by a window overlooking the pool.

There were a lot of gorgeous bodies out there, all of whom Suzie had been dissecting while they enjoyed their salads and drinks.

"Why aren't you looking forward to it?" "You know why. Becca."

"Becca?" Suzie frowned. "If anything, I thought you'd be ecstatic to be getting far, far away from the wicked witch. It's all you've been able to talk about for, like, ever."

"I know," Maddie said, playing with the food on her plate. "Now I'm not so sure."

"Why? Don't tell me you like her now and think you'll miss her."

Maddie smirked. "Not likely. I'm more worried about leaving her with my dad and grandpa."

Suzie nodded. "Ah. I see. You know what, though? They're grown men. They can take care of themselves."

"Can they?" Maddie didn't think so. "What's the worst that could happen?"

"I don't know—anything, knowing her. I feel like with every day that passes, she's more and more excited about me leaving. She's always resented me. You know that."

"Yes, just like you resent her. How's that Disney song go?

Tale as old as time…" Suzie laughed.

Maddie didn't laugh. She wasn't as tipsy as her friend obviously was. "I resent her because I know she doesn't care about my father. I don't give a care either way if she likes me. It's him. She tricked him into marrying her."

"Maddie. How did she do that? Let's get real. I know you've been telling yourself this for a long time, maybe to help you understand what happened. I think it was very simple. Your dad was lonely. Your mom had died a long time before then. He also wanted you to have a mother. Becca was a babe. She set her sights on him and reeled him in. I mean, come on. How many of our friends could say the same thing about their home life?" Suzie had a point. Most of their friends were from broken families.

"This feels different. She's…not a good person. I've always had that feeling. She wants so much, more than she has. She'll do anything to get it."

"What are you saying?" Suzie's voice dropped to a whisper. "Do you think she'd, like, hurt your dad?"

"I don't know," Maddie whispered, looking around to be sure nobody was listening in. "But I did a little research into her first husband's death…"

"Oh, Maddie, that's sick. You're morbid."

"Whatever. Do you want to hear what I found out or not?"
"Okay. What did you find, Sherlock?

"The coroner's report said there was cyanide in his bloodstream."

"What?" Suzie's eyes nearly popped out. "Okay, first, how did you get your hands on the coroner's report?"

"Never mind how." She'd paid a clerk to copy it for her. "The bottom line is ҭI did a little more digging online. About how a little bit of cyanide could kill a person. The concentration in his bloodstream wouldn't have been enough to kill him outright—but it would have been enough if the level had been steady for long enough. In other words, if he'd been ingesting it a little bit at a time over the course of many months."

"I don't know whether to be horrified by what you're saying or horrified by the lengths you're willing to go to," Suzie said, looking stunned.

"Don't you get it?"

"Oh, I totally get it. Believe me, this is crazy. But let's be reasonable. Even if she did kill her husband—and who knows if she actually did it—would she be stupid enough to try the same thing again? I mean, if she got away with it the first time, why would she press her luck a second time?"

"That's a good point," Maddie admitted. "I hadn't thought about it that way."

"Let's face it. The woman's a lot of things, but stupid isn't one of them. If I were her, I'd lay low for the rest of my life. She's got a good thing going with your dad. He's rich, gorgeous. That dark hair, the deep-set eyes…" Maddie made a face. Suzie shrugged, and continued, "Sorry, I know he's your dad, and it's weird to hear that, but he's a hottie."

"Gross."

"Then I guess you don't want to know how many of us had crushes on him growing up." "Oh, double gross!" Maddie cringed, and they both laughed.

"See what I mean, though? She has no reason to do anything like that now. She'd be killing the goose that laid the platinum eggs."

"Don't you mean golden eggs?" "No, those don't apply here." They both laughed.

Suzie could be a flake, but she was one of the smartest of Maddie's friends. Maddie felt better already.

"I think we're done eating, don't you?" Maddie asked. She signaled for the check. Suzie went for her purse, but Maddie stopped her. "My treat—or, rather, my father's."

"You mean your hot, sexy father?" "Oh, shut up."

Chapter 15

"What do you think of this?" Suzie stepped out of the dressing room, in a halter dress with a floaty, sexy skirt that just skimmed her knees. The coral color was a little last season, but it looked fantastic against her tanned skin and nearly white-blonde hair.

"It looks awesome on you," Maddie said. "You should get it. It would be great for a pool party, or maybe on a boat. I heard Jack Christiansen is having a late graduation party on his dad's yacht next month."

"Ooh, then I'm definitely getting this," Suzie giggled.

"I've wanted to get in Jack's pants for an entire year."

"I know. I'm pretty sure he does, too. You're not subtle."

"So why isn't he taking what's a sure thing?" Suzie pouted, untying the knot at the back of her neck, letting the dress fall to her feet.

"Because he was dating Willow up until, like, five minutes ago." Maddie raised an eyebrow at her friend.

Suzie frowned. "So?" Maddie laughed. Suzie never saw a problem with cheating.

"So he's still posting pics of them together on Facebook. It's pathetic. Do you really want a guy who obviously can't get over his ex-girlfriend?" Maddie asked.

"Hmm, maybe you're right. I hid him a long time ago since I kept seeing pics of the two of them together. Good call," Suzie said, then added, "Maybe I'll just sleep with him one time. Get it out of my system."

They both laughed. They'd been trying on outfits at the

boutique for two hours, without an end in sight. As soon as the salesgirls saw them walk in, they knew a juicy commission was in their immediate future.

One of them entered the dressing room with a bright smile on her face. "Would either of you care for a glass of champagne?" Suzie nodded behind the girl's back.

"Yes, we would. Thank you," Maddie said, waiting until the girl was gone before she giggled. "It's hilarious that they serve us without bothering to ask how old we are."

"They know how old we are," Suzie said, trying on a pair of jeans. "It's how old our plastic is that matters. They want to take care of us because our daddies take care of them, even if our daddies don't know it."

Something about what she said struck a nerve. "What made you say that?" Maddie asked. "What?"

"About our daddies not knowing."

"They don't, do they? I mean, you told your dad you were going shopping for school, right?" "Yeah…"

"And you're using his plastic today, right?" "Yeah…"

Suzie shrugged. "It's not rocket science."

Maddie gazed into the mirror, not seeing herself. Her thoughts were far away. "What's up?" Suzie was looking at her, hands on her slim hips.

"Nothing. It's just…Elix gave me a bunch of grief about that today."

"Oh, him. Mr. High and Mighty. Like he has room to talk." Suzie scoffed.

"Yeah, I know. It made me mad. Only…I think I was madder at myself than at him. I felt guilty." She turned to Suzie. "Do you ever feel guilty? Like, can't we just tell our dads we're using their money to go shopping? What's the big deal?"

"Maddie," Suzie pointed out. "We have to do *something*. Other kids our age are out there right now, scoring blow or shooting up. Trying to do anything they can to feel excited about something. You and I, we shop. And we keep it a secret because we want that thrill. That excitement."

"What makes you so insightful?"

"It's what my therapist says." She shrugged.

"And you don't care? I mean, you do it anyway?"

"Sure. Why not? There are plenty of worse things we could be doing with the money. Like scoring blow."

"I guess you're right." The salesgirl came in with two glasses of champagne, which Suzie happily downed. Maddie wasn't so enthusiastic.

Chapter 16

"You're a real pain in the butt. You know that?"

Elix turned, surprised. Maddie had finished shopping earlier than planned; her heart hadn't been in it, so she came straight home to give him a piece of her mind.

"What do you mean?" he asked, coming toward her. She was leaning on the fence that separated the area in which the horses grazed and the rest of the property. Elix had been tending to one of the horse's hooves when she found him.

He leaned on the opposite side of the fence, close to

Maddie. She smelled the horses and his sweat, mixed in with the chlorine from their earlier swim, on him,

She stared off, straight ahead, watching the horses. "I was all set to have a good time today with my friend. And you had to ruin it." "How did I ruin it?"

"By accusing me of stealing from my father." "I didn't mean to."

"Yes, you did." She sighed. "In a way, you were right. I'm not stealing cash from his wallet, but I'm using his money any way I want to without asking him about it, first. I know he'll never miss it. It's never bothered me before!" "What do you think that means?"

"I told you! It means you're a pain in the butt!"

Elix laughed. "I don't think so. If I'd come to you two years ago, accusing you of taking advantage of your father, you'd flip me off like you did earlier today." Maddie blushed, remembering. "Then you'd go shopping and not give it a second thought. You wouldn't care."

"So what are you trying to say? I'm…growing up?"

"Something like that, yeah." He grinned at her. "Welcome to an adult conscience. It sucks."

They laughed together. "I don't know, Elix. There's so much noise in my head right now. I feel like so much of my life is a joke, just a game. Fake. Lunches, dinners, playing nice with the kids of my dad's friends. It's all a big lie."

"What's not a lie? What do you like to do?"

Maddie bit her lip, thinking. "Playing tennis. Rowing." She'd been on championship teams in both sports throughout high school and planned to continue in college.

"Okay, that's a good start. What else?" "Riding Lady."

"That can be arranged. What else?"

She gave it some thought, then shrugged. "Hanging out with my friends. My real friends." She glanced at him, wishing she had the nerve to tell him she meant him, specifically. He was the only friend she had who always told her the truth. She could go to him with anything, and he never tried to make her feel bad. If she felt bad, she knew, it was because she'd done something wrong. All he did was shine a light on her conscience. It could be very uncomfortable, but it was what she needed.

"So those are the things you need to focus on. Think about those things this summer. Think about what you want to do for the rest of your life." He sighed, looking around. "There's a lot more to life than Halcyon. You'll find your place in it."

"So will you." His face darkened.

"It might take me a little longer," he said. She frowned, touching his arm. "Hey. You haven't ridden Lady yet today."

Maddie laughed. "In this?" She pointed to her designer dress.

"Who cares? Hike it up. Christ, that bathing suit you wore today had you practically naked."

"You're gross." Maddie climbed the fence, Elix holding his arms out to help her. She jumped, and he caught her. There was a breathless moment when he held her…then let her go.

"Come on," he said. "She was asking me about you." They walked together to where Lady stood, waiting.

Toni House

Chapter 17

Becca looked at herself in the full-length mirror on the back of the bathroom door.

Endless hours spent at the gym paid off. Her body looked nearly as good as it did before she had the boys. How many women could say they looked just as good as they had when they were eighteen?

All right—maybe her backside wasn't quite as high as it used to be. Maybe her breasts weren't as full. It was getting more difficult to keep the cellulite off her thighs. It wouldn't be long before she'd have to rely on liposuction, the way so many of her acquaintances did. She'd always prided herself on not needing anything but a brilliant trainer and a little willpower.

She turned, checking out her rear view. She still looked good for forty-two. She ran her hands over her rear, admiring how smooth it still was. Her legs were long and lean, a pair of nude stilettos making them appear longer. She turned again, running a hand over her flat stomach. A nearly carb- less life was worthwhile. Her breasts were heavy in her hands, pushed up and together by the exquisite lace bra she wore. Cleavage for days.

Her freshly blown-out hair was a rich, beautiful blonde thanks to Iris's genius. It made her green eyes sparkle over her full, pouty lips.

"Still got it," she murmured to herself, winking appreciatively. There was nothing like the feeling of power her looks and body gave her. Sometimes, they were all a woman had in a cold and unforgiving world. Becca had smarts, too, but when dealing with pigheaded chauvinists, it wasn't easy to get them to connect on an intellectual level. She wasn't above using every weapon at her disposal.

She took a deep breath, let it out, and then walked from the bathroom into the bedroom.

"Come here, you," he murmured, holding a hand out to her from where he sat on the bed. She went to him, taking her time, enticing him. The sight of her nearly-naked body was always enough to get him aroused. Glancing down, she saw his member already at half-mast.

"I want you so much," she whispered, standing between his open legs. His hands were immediately on her, skimming her small waist, her rounded hips. Digging into her butt. She giggled when he smacked her there, making her flesh jiggle.

"I want you," he replied in a desperate growl. His tongue licked her navel, then went lower. She gasped, tilting back her head and holding him to her as he licked her pelvis, then lower where her thighs met.

"You're so sexy," he whispered. His hands moved up her front, to her breasts. He breathed heavily, touching and holding them in his hands, squeezing them. She unhooked the back of her bra, letting the straps fall from her shoulders. As always, his eyes widened when her C-cup breasts broke free of their prison.

Becca guided his mouth to her. She sighed in pure pleasure as he latched on, greedily sucking one, then the other breast. The familiar ache started between her legs. "Mmm…you're the best…"

"I'll show you what else I'm best at." He took her by the waist, moving her to the bed. She reclined, one long leg on either side of him. When he sank to his knees, she sighed, knowing what was coming next.

He worked her panties slowly down her legs, and Becca closed her eyes. When his tongue made contact with her aching flesh, she groaned. He was the best when it came to this.

"Yes…Chip…oh, yes…"

Chip Davis grinned up at her from between her legs then went back to licking her most private parts. She closed her eyes, focusing on the pleasure her lawyer was giving her. She held his head in her hands, desperately trying to keep him closer to her core as he drove her higher and higher.

She needed more of him, had been craving him all week in fact. "Give it to me, baby…please…"

She rolled over, onto her hands and knees. She sighed in satisfaction when he slid inside her. Becca took control as she always did, pushing back against him. She moaned louder and louder as she felt a climax building within her.

"Yes! Yes! Oh, Chip!" She cried out his name, knowing he loved it when she did, as an orgasm wracked her. He waited while she came down from her bliss, stroking her back and thighs as she caught her breath. Once she recovered, she rolled onto her back, taking him inside her again. Now

Becca wrapped her legs around him, pulling him closer and closer.

"That's right… yes…" she whispered in his ear. She raked her perfectly manicured nails down his back, gripping his rear as he rode her harder. He grunted, panted, and moaned like an animal. She reveled in it, begging him to give her more. The thickness moving in and out made the pressure build again, more quickly this time. She moved with him, working for it, wanting it.

This time they came together, filling the room with lustful noise. "Chip…oh, God…you're so good…" He moaned in appreciation. In truth, he wasn't the very best, but he was good enough. She'd needed the release. When he pushed himself up on his arms, grinning down at her, she grinned back and kissed him lightly.

He rolled off, getting up to take a shower. Becca sat up, making herself comfortable on the bed while he sang quietly off-key. She'd never had any problem with infidelity—it was all she'd known during both her first and current marriage. There was no reason for a beautiful, sensual woman to go without. She refused to become some overstressed, undersexed harpy. She'd been meeting Chip like this, at the Four Seasons once every other week for a year.

There were other perks. Chip, for example, was one of the

best lawyers on the East coast. He had the answers she needed at the moment.

The shower was turned off. Becca watched as he crossed the room, his damp body glistening before he toweled it off. He was toned, firm, disciplined. His dark brown hair had a touch of gray at the temples though he was barely out of his thirties. Funny how men looked more handsome with a touch of gray, while she'd just come from having hers covered up for fear of looking like a hag.

She'd arranged herself carefully, trying to look as fetching as possible. "You look worried," he said. As she knew he would.

"What? Oh. I have a lot on my mind, I guess." She looked away, toward the window.

"What's the matter? Tell me." He dropped the towel to the floor, climbing in beside her. He wrapped one arm around her, pulling her close. She let her head drop to his chest.

"Chip, I've been so unhappy lately. For years, come to think of it. It's all becoming too much." "What is?"

"The lies. The way I have to pretend to be happy when I'm not."

"I know you're not happy right now. You're having a hard time with Maddie and the boys are no picnic." Their lawyer was one of the few people who knew exactly the trouble Cal and Rory got into, as it was he who inevitably got them out of it. "It will pass, though. Once Maddie's out of the house you'll be able to breathe again, right?"

"Will I?" She sighed dramatically. "What's that mean?"

She let a tearful tone sneak in. "Mac's the most miserable human being I've ever known."

Chip laughed. "He's a stubborn old goat, isn't he? But a strong man. Not a man to play games with." "He's a nasty, foul-mouthed old man who disrespects me every chance he gets."

"Come on, now." He squeezed her. Becca was glad he couldn't see her eyes as she rolled them in her head. If she'd wanted reassurances, she'd have gone to her daddy for advice. If he was still alive.

She sighed again, getting to the point. "When he's gone—and I'm not saying that will be any time soon, because he won't ever die—everything goes to JT. Right?"

"I believe so. It's been a while since I've reviewed the will, but as far as I know, that's how he's set it up."

"Mm-hmm. And if something were to happen to JT?"

Chip froze. Becca felt it. She shouldn't have pushed so hard. "What do you mean, if something happened to JT?"

She sat up, eyes wide. "I was only trying to prove a point. If something happened to JT, I would only get a few thousand dollars. Right? So would my boys."

Chip's eyes narrowed thoughtfully. "That's right. Again, it's been a while. From what I remember, everything's set up to go to Maddie."

Maddie. Always Maddie. "That's what I mean. He's left us no security whatsoever. I'm trapped. I have to play happy wife when I wonder if something's going to happen to him every day."

"Becca, sweetheart, what could happen to him? He's a young man, a vital man. Don't be so negative. While you're married, you're set. The best of everything."

"What if he gets tired of me some day?" This was a very real concern of hers, one she'd never voiced before now. She knew he had a roaming eye, just as she did. What if he decided he was through pretending their marriage had been a good idea? Now that Maddie was nearly grown, there was no need to keep the figurehead of a mother around the house. He could throw her out in an instant.

"Who could get tired of you? Just look at you. You're the most delicious, sexiest woman in the world. You'll have him wrapped around your finger 'til the day he dies."

She sighed impatiently. "That's not true. He hates me."

"Honey." She allowed him to pull her close again. This wasn't the way she'd planned for their conversation to go at all. She'd wanted sympathy, not advice.

"Besides," Chip continued, "didn't Frank leave you pretty well set up when he died? Ten million dollars, wasn't it?"

It's not enough. "Yes, that was the amount."

"Did you invest it, the way your advisor said?" Becca nodded. "Then it's all right. You'll be taken care of for the rest of your life."

"That's not enough money." Her true colors were showing now. She didn't care. She was frustrated, and maybe a little tipsy still.

He froze again. "For some people that would be more than enough to be happy for a very long time."

"I'm not some people." She tilted back her head, meeting his blue eyes. "And neither are you. Don't pretend you are. Otherwise, you wouldn't charge the outrageous fees my husband happily pays."

He chuckled softly, taking her chin in his hands. "All right, so we're both greedy money grabbers. Maybe that's why we're so attracted to each other in the first place. What of it?"

"Don't pretend I don't have a point, is all. You know what

I mean. I need a way to provide for myself. To make all this worth it, in case something happens with JT."

Chip's hand tightened, now nearly encompassing her throat. "If you're saying what I think you're saying, you need to take a step back. Hurting that man would be the biggest mistake of your life."

She smiled. "Chip. What are you talking about?"

"You know what I'm talking about. I'd hate to see a man I respect fall ill out of nowhere."

Her eyes widened. She didn't like the way he was holding her throat. "No, I don't know what you mean. I suggest you let go of me."

He did, smirking. "You're not quite as smart as you think you are, beautiful. Don't make the mistake of thinking nobody questioned the way Frank died. Let that be enough for you, the fact you got away with it."

"I won't dignify that with a response." She climbed from the bed, not bothering to wrap herself in a sheet before crossing the room to the chair where she'd hung her clothes.

"No need. You and I both know what you did. And hey—that's your business. What's done is done. Just don't think you'll get away with doing it again. Believe me, the moment that man comes to me with a request to change his will in your favor, I'm going to question his motives. Right before I strongly suggest he hire a professional food taster and a bodyguard."

Her back was to him, so he couldn't see the look of pure hatred on her face. The smug jerk. It looked as though this would be their last meeting at the hotel.

The bed springs squeaked as he got up and crossed the room to place his hands on her shoulders. "Now, don't go away angry. Come on. If anything, isn't it nice to be able to be yourself in front of somebody? You don't have to pretend with me. I know who you are, what you are. And it doesn't bother me one bit. We have fun together. Let's not ruin that."

Becca shook off his hands, turning to face him. "You're

smug, and conceited. I refuse to involve myself with a man who has these disgusting ideas about me. From now on, our relationship is purely professional."

He laughed. "Have it your way. Take the high road, as though you have the right. Just watch your back, Mrs. Rossi. Don't think I won't have my eye on you from now on."

"I'd think you'd be too busy making deals with opposing lawyers to drag cases out longer than they need to be, just so you both can keep charging your clients for the time spent." His smile dimmed. "I don't know much about the law, but wouldn't something like that get you into trouble? I mean, if word got out?"

"What proof would you have?"

"I might not have proof, but the court of public opinion doesn't need proof, does it? The right words whispered in the right ears will start a fire that will burn your firm to the ground, and you with it." She turned. "Zip me, please."

She'd have to give Iris an even bigger tip next time she

saw her, out of thanks for providing that bit of gossip. That's all it had been—gossip. Chip's reaction had turned it into something else.

She slid behind the wheel of the Porsche minutes later, gunning the engine before peeling out. She'd burned that bridge. It was no good convincing JT to change his will unless they changed attorneys.

If they did, Chip might open his mouth out of spite toward her.

There were no backup plans. All she could do was go with Plan Number One: Destroy JT and take over the company.

Toni House

Chapter 18

The week went by in a flash. Before JT knew it, the day of the Board meeting had come. He'd dreaded it somewhat, but he felt confident after reviewing the reports. He had a foolproof set of numbers to deliver to the board. They couldn't have a single complaint.

They were a tough crowd, all long-time members of the board of Henry Enterprises. JT respected the amount of experience they had. These men had been through the ups and downs of a fluctuating economy, a boom and bust real estate market. The decisions they made with Mac at the head of the table had contributed to the success of Henry

Enterprises.

They saw JT as an imposter. He was a young upstart benefitting from nepotism, at least in their eyes.

When Mac had set JT in his place, once it became clear the old man's declining health would make it impossible to serve as he once had, there had been a nearly insulting amount of grumbling. Mac's

word was final, as anyone who'd ever faced him knew well. There was no getting him to back down.

JT had been left to deal with the aftermath. The fall of the real estate market occurring around the same time hadn't helped. It had been a struggle to keep Henry Enterprises at the top of the heap, but JT had managed it—with Mac as his most trusted advisor.

He strode into the boardroom, the picture of a self-possessed billionaire. The ten board members were waiting, five on either side of the table. JT estimated their combined age to be somewhere between six hundred and seven fifty.

"Good morning, gentleman." He settled into his chair, straightening his jacket and tie. "Shall we get started? I'm eager to hear your thoughts on the most recent financials."

"I have a piece of business to bring to the Board," one of the men interjected. JT stifled an exasperated sigh. Why were they always trying to talk over him?

"Can it wait until we cover the business on our agenda, Mark?" "It cannot." The rest of them men murmured their agreement. "What is this?" They all seemed to know something JT didn't.

Mark continued. "I shared this with the other board members prior to your arrival, JT. One of my sources shared a rather distressing bit of news with me yesterday, which I've had an investigator explore since."

"An investigator? Why not bring this to me yourself, and allow me to explore it?"

"I felt it wasn't worth broaching here without some reasonable amount of certainty." JT's blood pressure rose. "And?"

"And it looks as though some anonymous source is determined to buy out Henry Enterprises."

JT's immediate reaction was to laugh in disbelief. It wasn't possible. "That's like a child saying they want to buy the moon." He was gratified to hear chuckling around the table.

Alexander, one of the oldest and sagest men in the room, spoke. "That's very similar to my initial response—to all of our reactions, in fact." The board members murmured their agreement. "However, it's not impossible."

"A buyout. Who would be so underhanded as to not come right out and announce their intentions?" He looked around the table. "Any ideas?"

The men looked uncomfortable. Finally, Mark spoke. "My investigator couldn't find out anything concrete, but the truth is…Mac didn't make many friends over the years."

"I'd guessed as much. I do live with the man." More chuckling from the board members. Mark continued. "There's one man in particular with whom Mac always butted heads."

"He felt as though he should have had a bigger piece of the Henry pie," Alexander interjected. "In fact…he felt as though Mac cheated him out of his share of Henry Enterprises."

"Wait—Mac had a partner?" Why hadn't he ever told JT of this?

"They could have been. They could even have come to some sort of verbal agreement. Mac would never speak of it." Typical. Whenever there was a topic of conversation Mac didn't feel comfortable addressing, he clammed up.

JT cleared his throat. "So what you're telling me is…the company could be in jeopardy." The men exchanged uncomfortable glances, then nodded.

JT absorbed this blow, unwilling to let the board members see him sweat. "Wonderful. Well, I'm glad to have such positive numbers to share with you in light of that news."
It was good to know he'd worked so hard to keep the company on top so another man could swoop in and reap

the rewards.

***

The meeting couldn't have ended soon enough. Pressley had scheduled JT's lunch with Stephen for that afternoon. Lunch with an old friend would help him decompress.

Sitting in the back of the town car, JT fumed. Who did this person think they were, whoever they were? Henry Enterprises wasn't a name to be taken lightly. JT Rossi wasn't, either.

He'd never felt more protective of anything besides Maddie. In a way the company was like his child too. He'd worked his butt off for nearly twenty years, building and nurturing it. Struggling through all the growing pains, the down economy and the crazy impact the up and down oil prices have on everything. All for what? For some greedy pig to come in and take it from him?

JT's eyes narrowed. Nobody did that and got away with it.

***

Stephen was waiting for him when he arrived at the restaurant. They hadn't seen each other in more than three years, they were both busy with their respective careers. Stephen was on his third term in the Senate, and one of the favorites of his constituents and the media alike. With his All-American good looks, excellent breeding, and beautiful family, he was the perfect politician.

"Marlowe, you don't look a day over sixty," JT said as he sat down.

"And you look like a man who sleeps remarkably well at night for all the crooked business deals he transacts," Stephen coolly replied. They laughed.

"How's it been so long?" JT asked. "Busy men living busy lives." "How's Bethany?"

"The same as always. A frigid, Botoxed WASP whose idea of having fun in the sack is doing it with the lights on."

"But she makes the ideal Senator's wife!" JT pointed out. "Which is why we're still together. And Becca?"

"The same as always. A beautiful, demanding wife who thinks I don't know how much sleeping around she does." JT enjoyed the first taste of his Scotch, letting it warm him after the morning he'd had.

"That's something the two of you have in common," Stephen joked with a wink.

"You should talk. JFK's probably the only politician who scored more tail than you do." "And Maddie?"

"Perfection. Going to Cornell in the fall." He felt his face light up as he spoke of her. The one true, pure thing in his life.

"You must be proud."

JT heard the sour note in his friend's voice. "What's wrong? Something with Bobby?"

Stephen grimaced. "He's been keeping our lawyers busy lately. Something about a girl, some assault accusations…" JT frowned. This wasn't the first time Bobby Marlowe had come under fire after a girl claimed he'd assaulted her. Stephen's son was the one area in which JT always felt he had to bite his tongue, otherwise he would have recommended institutionalization long ago. The kid was little more than an animal, using his father's name and money to abuse others. He was the kind of person who pulled the wings off butterflies.

JT changed the subject. "So what was it you wanted to talk about? I mean, this is the first time you've cleared room in your schedule for me in three years. I figured it must be important."

"It is." Stephen's face instantly became animated. "I have it in good faith that some large tracts of land are about to skyrocket in value. You know how the government's been pouring money into public works projects, museums, that sort of thing?"

"Yeah, I'd read about it."

"The land surrounding these building projects would naturally go up in value, right?"

"Of course it would. But the final list of projects hasn't

been released yet. The locations are still up in the air." He looked at his friend, knowing from the smirk on his face that this wasn't true.

Stephen grinned. "The list is out there. It just hasn't been released, as you say. And it won't be released for another three months."

"So you're saying…"

"I'm saying a savvy real estate executive might want to snap up that land before the value goes through the roof."

JT was intrigued, despite the qualms he felt. "It would have to be done carefully. Holding companies would need to be set up. Otherwise anyone could connect the two of us."

"I have it all figured out. Believe me, I've been doing my research."

JT scanned the surrounding area with his eyes. The other diners murmured discreetly, lost in their own conversations. "You want a piece of the profit. That's what you're telling me."

"And why not? Consider it a finder's fee." Stephen chuckled.

"It's worth thinking over," JT admitted.

"Think fast. We have a lot of work to do in a short amount of time." The waiter approached to take their order. They switched topics after that, doing the sort of chatting old friends do when they get together to catch up. The proposed deal was never far from JT's mind.

Chapter 19

Becca popped her head in through the door. "JT, honey, can I have a minute?"

He was at his desk in his home office. Jeez, did he ever stop working? When they first met, years ago, she'd thought his dedication to the company was sexy. He had maintained Mac's legacy once it was clear his health wasn't what it used to be. Mac had only just started slipping in those days, a slight stroke making it difficult for him to rule with the iron first that had made him famous.

Now, Becca found her husband's workaholic tendencies irritating. She'd never had real feelings for him—or for any man—so it was impossible to look on him the way she knew some wives looked on their husbands. As poor overworked dears, sweating all day to provide for their families.

He glanced up at her from the stack of papers on his desk. "If it's a quick minute, honey. I have a ton of contracts to review here." It didn't look like contracts, even to Becca's inexperienced eye. He was looking through a pile of old papers. Was he hiding something from her?

"What's the point of having an assistant if you have to do all the grunt work yourself?" She didn't imagine the way he flinched when she mentioned Pressle, a girl younger than herself who bore a passing resemblance to Madaline. He was so transparent.

"She's not qualified to do this."

"Then your other employees. I mean, really, JT. You're working yourself into an early grave."

"Is this what you came in here for? To nag me over my work habits?" He was sharp, tenser than usual.

She shook her head, perching gracefully on the one uncovered corner of his desk. "Of course not. Sorry. I was hoping to talk about Maddie's birthday."

"This again?" His exasperation wasn't unwarranted. They'd been battling over whether or not to throw a party ever since the incident with the blowout Maddie threw when her parents were out of town.

"You might be happy to know I was coming in to suggest we host the party, after all."

JT's dark eyes widened in surprise, the contracts forgotten momentarily. As always, the mention of his daughter was enough to get him away from his work. "Really? What changed your mind?"

She shrugged. "I don't know. It all seems so arbitrary in the face of the big picture, doesn't it? I mean, the girl's going off to college in a couple of months. We didn't throw a graduation party since her birthday fell so close.

We should give her a little something for having worked so hard in high school, to celebrate her. One little transgression shouldn't ruin that."

His handsome face broke into a wide smile. She could have loved him, once. He was dashing, smart, sexy. Her eyes had been too fixed on the prize, however. And by the time she realized how little she'd get if their marriage ever ended, whether by divorce or death, it was too late. She'd promised him the moon and stars.

"I'm so happy to hear you say that. I know Maddie will be, too." *I'm sure she will, selfish little brat.*

Becca smiled. "I wanted to talk it over with you ⹁before dinner. I thought we might bring it up at the table."

He smiled again, standing to wrap his arms around her. He always smelled good. His arms were strong and warm. He had a kind heart. Why couldn't she love him?

"Thank you. I'm sure this will make Maddie very happy," he murmured. Becca's heart hardened, as it always did against her stepdaughter.

"I know it will. I'm glad it makes you happy, too." She extracted herself, turning to leave the office.

"Dinner's in thirty minutes. Don't keep Mac waiting." The sound of JT's chuckle followed her out of the room. She'd nearly closed the door behind her when she heard him call to her.

"Yes?"

"Come back, please. Shut the door."

Becca couldn't hide her surprise. She returned to where he stood, waiting expectantly. "I got some unsettling news from the Board today." He motioned for her to have a seat. "What is it?"

"One of Mac's old rivals is preparing for a takeover."

"A takeover?" Becca's mind whirled. "Who has the resources for something like that?" "A man obsessed with taking Mac down, from what I understand."

She couldn't blame a person for the impulse. She'd wanted

to take him down for years. "Do you know anything about him?"

"I'm looking into it." He referenced the stack of papers on his desk.

"Honey, I wouldn't worry too much about it yet. There's no guarantee this will pan out. I'm sure Mac burned plenty of bridges over the years. It's one thing to say you want to have revenge on the man who wronged you, but another to go through with it. Besides, this mystery person is probably, what, a hundred years old?" He chuckled, and she smiled. "Don't let it get to you until you find out more. Nothing big can happen without you knowing about it."

She left the room, a secret smile spreading over her face. It looked like there was another person in the world who wanted exactly what she did. Maybe she'd have to do a little digging of her own, shake the man's hand and ask if he needed any help. Maybe she'd get a piece of the spoils for herself.

Chapter 20

Becca raised a glass of wine to her lips, observing her little family over the rim. JT caught her eye, and she nodded slightly. Now was the time.

"Maddie? We were wondering if we could talk with you about something."

"What is it, Daddy?" Maddie didn't look at her stepmother. She never did unless she had to, Becca noticed. Maybe because they understood each other so well.

JT beamed at Becca, who managed to crack a smile in

return. "Your mama and I were talking, and we decided it would be a good idea for us to throw you a birthday party, after all."

Maddie gasped. "You did? What made you change your minds?" JT nodded toward Becca, forcing Maddie to look her in the eye. Becca smiled benevolently.

"We thought it would be a nice way to send you off to college. You deserve it. You worked so hard to get where you are. Plus, a girl only turns eighteen once. You deserve a memorable party." She stroked Maddie's hair, patted her cheek.

"This is awesome!" The girl turned back to her father, then beamed at her grandfather. "Isn't this awesome?"

"A bunch of screaming teenagers, tearing my house up? Yes, that's awesome." He was barely concealing a smile. Becca knew from experience the old man would grant his granddaughter anything she wanted. She could ask to burn the place down, and he'd hand her a pack of matches.

"We'll behave, I promise." Maddie giggled.

"You'd better." JT's tone was stern now. "No messing around. No funny business."

"Funny business? Exactly what would that be?" Oh, that pert sense of humor. It never ceased to make Becca's skin crawl.

"He means no screwing around with the boys," Mac blurted out. Even Becca had to stifle a snort. "Mac!" JT's olive complexion turned red.

"Daddy, I'm practically an adult. I can hear things like that without them ruining me forever." Maddie turned to Mac. "I promise, Grandpa. No…effing around." She patted his hand.

"No drinking, either." "*Daddy!*"

"I mean it. I won't have illegal drinking in this house. I won't be held responsible for your friends getting behind the wheel drunk, either. I know you kids think you can handle it, but you can't. That's final." Becca knew he meant it, though she knew it was a waste of a speech. Kids would always find a way to drink at a party. In a house as big as Halcyon with the surrounding grounds, a little sneaking around was inevitable. Maddie pouted, her arms crossed.

"Madaline," Becca said, "your father and I are meeting you halfway by even throwing you a party. The least you can do is meet us halfway." She saw JT's grateful smile from the corner of her eye. He loved it when she played Concerned Stepmother.

This did little to endear her in Maddie's eyes, but then what did that matter? She hated the little brat. "Fine. No drinking. God, how lame. Nobody will want to come."

"Maybe they're not your friends, then," Mac said. For once, the old man had a point. That was enough to shut Maddie up.

"Don't let this get you all worked up, sweetheart. This was supposed to be a happy announcement. Why don't we sit down to work on a guest list as soon as you have the chance? I can have invitations ordered tomorrow." Becca was smiling at her stepdaughter, who rewarded her with a raised eyebrow. Naturally, she'd question the motives behind this show of attention. She wasn't completely stupid.

Maddie shrugged. "All right. We can do it tonight if you want." Becca nodded with a smile, then winked at JT. Her eyes fell on Mac, who looked even more suspicious than Maddie had. Of course , he would. He never missed a thing, senile or not.

Sure enough, as soon as the plates were cleared from the table and they stood, Mac caught Becca's eye. She knew this meant he wanted to have a word.

"Where's this sudden show of affection coming from?" he asked, smiling. *Like the cat that ate the canary,* Becca thought.

"Mac, I'm tired of your scheming and conniving."

"My scheming?" He laughed. "My girl, I'm an amateur compared to you. I know you never offer to do anything solely out of the goodness of your heart. So what is it? What are you trying to gain from this?"

"A little peace, maybe. Did you ever think of that?"

He shook his head. "No. Try again. More convincing, this time."

"I'm sorry that isn't good enough for you. But you and my husband both seem to suffer from the same delusion that Maddie can do no wrong. I'm the only one who sees how manipulative she can be."

"Oh no, dear. That's where you're wrong. I see her for exactly who she is, just like I see you for who you are. I might be getting old; I might be forgetful, but I still see everything."

Becca sized him up, weighing his words. "Why do you let her get away with it, then?"

"Because she's a headstrong little girl. She's going to find a way to get what she wants. But she's not a bad girl. There's a difference." He smirked. "She's not like you."

Becca turned on her heel and stormed out of the dining room. The old monster. He couldn't die fast enough for her liking.

Chapter 21

Becca and Maddie sat in the library, tellingly far from one another. Becca sat at the desk she used for correspondence, with her laptop open. Maddie sat halfway across the room, scrolling through her iPad.

"Could you pay a little bit of attention, dear? I'm doing this for you." It was like pulling teeth, getting a list of names from this girl. "I thought you were happy about the party. It doesn't seem that way, now."

"I'm sorry. It's just I'm going through my list of friends to decide who's worth an invite." "Your list of friends?"

Becca scoffed. "Is it really that long?"

Maddie scowled. "I have over thirteen-hundred friends, thank you."

"What? Where are these imaginary friends?" Maddie turned her tablet toward Becca with a smirk, revealing her Facebook friends list.

"Oh, you must be kidding," Becca laughed. "Facebook? That doesn't count."

"These are all people from school. Mostly, anyway. It's not like we've never met."

Becca shook her head, going through her own address list to create the guest list. "When I was your age, I had an address book. It was very simple."

"That was an awfully long time ago, wasn't it?" Becca shot her a warning look.

"Do you even have addresses for these people?" Becca asked. "Or were you planning on sending an invite via

Facebook? Very classy."

"I'm sure we can find their addresses. Isn't that what Daddy has an assistant for?" Becca bristled again. While she had spent the afternoon in bed with the lawyer, she didn't enjoy the reminder of her husband's infidelity. She couldn't prove it, but she was pretty certain Maddie only brought it up to rub her face in it.

Be nice, she reminded herself silently. *Remember the bigger picture*. The entire reason for throwing this party was to create the illusion of one, big, happy family. She had to start a case history of the times when she'd been a good stepmother, extending an olive branch to her willful stepdaughter.

People had to believe Becca had spent years trying to make the best of a difficult situation.

Becca nodded. "You're right, of course. That's a good idea." Maddie looked suspicious but stayed silent. She rose, bringing her tablet with her.

"Okay. I created a separate group of friends to make a list

of only those I want to invite." Becca scanned it.

"Over one hundred?" She looked at Maddie, and the girl shrugged.

"I'd be insulting them if I didn't. Besides, I know a bunch of them would be invited with their parents, anyway." Becca saw she had a point, recognizing many of the names from her own list.

Maddie leaned over Becca's shoulder, looking at the list on the screen. "Oh, the senator? Please tell me we're not inviting his entire family."

Becca looked at the entry in question. "Of course, we would. You just said it yourself. It would be an insult. The family's been close with them for years." "Not Bobby, though? Please?"

"Madaline Rossi, there's no way to invite the parents but forbid the son."

"He's a pervert, though." Maddie wrapped her arms around her midsection, biting her lip. "Oh, stop being such a drama queen." Becca turned back to the laptop.

"I mean it. He looks at me funny."

"Maybe if you didn't always wear dresses that left your boobs half hanging out when we went out with the family," Becca said, her voice cool.

"You should talk," Maddie retorted.

Becca was just opening her mouth to remind her stepdaughter who she was speaking to when one of the staff rushed into the room.

"Mrs. Rossi! Come quickly!"

"What is it?" Becca bolted out of her seat.

"It's old Mr. Henry. He's very sick!" The woman ran from the room, followed closely by Maddie, who had taken off running.

Becca closed her eyes briefly before following them. Maybe things were finally turning around, after all.

Toni House

138

Chapter 22

This again?

Mac had been feeling fine—more than fine, actually. He always felt good after giving that horrible woman a verbal takedown. It left him energized, pleased with himself.

He'd gone to his room, slowly as always. One of the main reasons why he always got to the table first and left last was his unwillingness to allow the rest of the family see him needing help to get around. He knew they knew…but they didn't need to see.

His faithful butler had helped him up the stairs, as he had

been doing ever since the first mini-stroke had left Mac unable to walk as well as he once had.

"Will you need anything tonight, Mr. Henry?"

"William, how many times do we need to have this conversation? Call me Mac, I'm telling you. Christ, they call *me* senile."

"And as I tell you every time, Mr. Henry, I don't feel right doing that. It feels disrespectful, somehow."

"Disrespectful? I'm the one telling you to do it." "All right, Mr. Henry. I'll try my best."

William had helped Mac to his room, where Mac got dressed for bed. He wasn't planning to go to sleep, per se, but it was stupid for a man his age to spend even an extra minute not being as comfortable as possible. Besides, who was he kidding? He wasn't going anywhere else tonight.

Once changed, he'd gotten into bed with the remote control and a book. His eyes were failing, but Maddie had bought him one of those e-reader gadgets. She showed him how to make the text larger, even backlight it so he could more easily read it. The things they came up with these days. He could have built his business three times as fast if he'd had this sort of technology at his fingertips back in the day.

He'd been having difficulty concentrating on his book, however. Not because he wasn't following along— sometimes he had to go back and re-read entire pages—but because his mind was on other matters.

What was that witch downstairs up to now?

She'd never once done something nice for Maddie or even stuck up for her in an argument if there wasn't something in it for her. Mac searched his admittedly failing memory for some idea of what she was angling for. Showing off to friends? That was a possibility. He'd known about her lunch date earlier in the day. Odds were the catty trophy wives she spent her time with had shown her up in some way and Becca felt she needed to reassert her position as Queen of the pack. He knew this house, *his* house, would be packed to the rafters with people and decked out like they were celebrating a visit from the President.

He wanted to believe this, but his instincts told him otherwise. She'd been overly nice, overly caring. There was something else going on.

Mac knew JT humored him, now that his faculties were failing. It was a mistake. A man didn't live to be as old as he had without picking up a thing or two. It would do his son-in-law well to pay attention to the wisdom of his elders. But Mac knew that when he'd been JT's age, he was just as single-minded. Focused on business with the rest of the world falling by the wayside. Mac noticed Maddie hadn't returned her father's platinum card at dinner as she'd promised. Did JT remember that promise? Probably not. His mind was on his work.

If JT's wife were a kind, sweet, caring girl like Mac's wife had been, he wouldn't have worried. Corrine was the model of what the wife of an ambitious man should be: sweet, intelligent but not overly so, beautiful, cultured, and able to hold her own in conversation with anyone from the lowliest employee to the richest, most powerful business partner. She'd allowed Mac the luxury of believing he ran his household, when they both knew she was the one in charge. Corrine had been from good Southern stock, raised to oversee a sprawling estate while making it appear as though she didn't have a thought in her head. She was the perfect match for him.

She was also steely strong when the time came. His wife had been his most trusted advisor. Many late nights were spent talking about deals, employee negotiations, and plans for expansion. She was well-read and gave informed opinions, helping Mac see sides to a situation he hadn't even imagined. She'd left him far too soon, even before Madaline did.

Madaline. His beautiful daughter and Maddie reminded Mac so much of his wife that sometimes it caused him physical pain. A look, a turn of phrase. Her laugh was nearly identical, her eyes even more so. His daughter had left him far too soon too.

The doctor had warned her it would be a difficult pregnancy, Mac remembered. She was on bedrest the entire second half, in fact. He'd advised a scheduled C-section as soon as the baby reached thirty-six weeks. Maddie had come into the world after thirty-five weeks and four days. Madaline had died immediately after the birth, a brain hemorrhage taking her quickly. She never held her daughter.

Maddie needed a mother. She still did, the stepmother JT chose never scratched the surface of what a mother should be. Maddie had grown up even more headstrong than her mother was as a young girl. JT was a good father, a loving one, but he wasn't able to provide the guidance a mother could have.

Becca didn't have a motherly bone in her body. Look at the way those two baboons of hers had turned out. Mac had known Frank Depure. He was a good man, a smart man. From a good family. He had his head turned by a flashy little piece of tail. Mac remembered Becca in those days; she'd been heart-stoppingly beautiful.

Frank's sons should have turned out to be good men. Instead, they were loafers, freeloaders, and spoiled brats who ran around getting into nonstop trouble. Cal had already been taken to task over a drinking problem—no surprise, seeing the way his mother downed her liquor. He'd wrecked two cars, even facing a lawsuit after hitting another car in the second crash. JT's lawyer had settled out of court. Rory had been involved with a stripper from some club, running away to Vegas to get married. JT had gotten the marriage annulled.

The two boys didn't have three brain cells between them. No, Becca had not done a good job of raising them.

Mac couldn't blame the boys entirely. It was her fault for being more interested in money and herself than her family. Oh, the way she'd begged JT to adopt her boys after getting married. You'd have thought she was the Virgin Mary herself, begging for the welfare of her sons. They needed a father, a proper father, and a good name. Mac had known even then she was only interested in securing their name and, ideally, getting money from JT. They'd get a lot further in life with the name Rossi. The poor boy had no idea. She'd overwhelmed him.

Mac had been thinking about all of this and more as he sat up in bed against his pillows. He'd put the e-reader aside, giving up. He'd had to pee. The last thing he remembered was swinging his legs out of bed and stepping onto the floor.

Then he woke up like this.

He couldn't speak. The words were forming in his head as always, but when he opened his mouth, gibberish came out. It was like some translator was stuck in his throat, changing what should have been clear speech to nothing. He knew what this was. He'd been the same way after his first stroke. Only it hadn't been this severe.

He looked around the hospital room, at the faces surrounding his bed. JT, looking stern and stoic. Maddie, tear-stained. Becca, triumphant.

"Oh, Grandpa. I'm so glad you're awake!" Maddie was sobbing, her head on Mac's shoulder. He tried to lift a hand to comfort her, pat her head, something. His hand only fluttered weakly. Hell's bells. Was it this bad?

"Mac," JT said, coming closer. "Do you know what happened to you?" Mac did his best, struggling to nod his head. It was enough, judging from JT's reaction.

"You understand you're in the hospital?" He nodded again. "And you hear me clearly?" A nod. "Thank God,"

Maddie mumbled, her voice thick with tears.

Mac's eyes fell on Becca, who stared back at him. She wasn't happy he'd woken up, not a bit. But the harpy still felt as though she had the upper hand, now. He knew she saw herself one step closer to having her mitts around the family fortune. Let her keep thinking that.

"I can't believe this," Maddie cried. "Here we were, planning a party. Like a party even matters. All the while, you were probably on the floor of your room. Can you ever forgive me?" There was nothing to forgive. He moved his head against hers, wanting her to look at him. She raised her head. He nodded, did his best to smile.

"Maddie, dear, it wasn't your fault. I'm sure your grandfather would want you to know that. Right, Mr. Henry?" Mac didn't look at Becca, only at Maddie. He nodded again.

This would have to happen now of all times. When he was so sure that woman had something up her sleeve, something that might threaten his Maddie. He'd have to find some way to communicate, eventually. For now, he was exhausted from simply having nodded his head a few times. His eyes started to close.

"We'll leave you alone to get some rest, now," JT said. Mac heard them all leaving his private room, JT murmuring reassurances to Maddie as they left.

He heard her breathing. Becca. She was still there, lingering at his bedside. He didn't have the strength to open his eyes. Maybe she thought he was already asleep.

"Sweet dreams, old man," Her whisper was menacing, deadly. He was surer than ever than somebody needed to stop her.

Chapter 23

JT was in his home office. He didn't have it in him to face the concern of the entire company right now.

It was bad enough that the board was on his back about this potential takeover. Now that Mac was sick, there was no way to tell how far their faith had fallen. They knew how he depended on Mac as an advisor. It wasn't as though he couldn't make his own decisions, though. Mac merely backed up the choices JT had already made.

They wouldn't want to hear that. A bunch of greedy, short-sighted old men. The one thing JT had wanted to do that

Mac had vetoed was find a new board of younger, fresher faces who could see the way business was changing. This wasn't the world of fifty or even twenty years ago. So much had changed since then. The entire world landscape had changed regarding business. None of the old men wanted to hear that. With Mac gone, the little confidence they had in JT would likely vanish.

He knew he only had so many days during which a family emergency would excuse him from being present in the office. Soon they'd all be wondering why he was hiding and probably assume it was out of a lack of confidence in his leadership. He couldn't afford to look weak.

He was eating himself up from the inside out. His ulcer burned. Was success worth this sort of grief? No wonder Mac had suffered a stroke before he turned sixty-five.

Now, here was the second stroke. He refused to give up, the old pirate. JT smiled fondly to himself. He had always looked at Mac as a father figure. He'd never had much of one in his life before marrying Madaline.

Mac hadn't approved when his daughter first brought her

new boyfriend home. JT was only in an upper-crust school, one a girl like Madaline would attend, because his mother had married an oil baron four years after JT's father abandoned them. To say he'd spend his formative years in less- than-ideal conditions would be an understatement. It was nearly squalor. His stepfather had saved them from the gutter.

But he wasn't a real father, always too busy to spend time on his stepson. JT felt like an afterthought. It was a great disappointment, since he'd dreamed that when his mother remarried he'd finally have the father he'd missed for so long.

Mac hadn't approved of him during that first meeting. JT wasn't from a good family. "Rossi," he'd sneered, right in front of JT. "What kind of last name is that?"

"It's my last name, sir," JT replied. Madaline had squeezed his hand, encouraging him. "I mean, where's it come from?"

"Where do last names come from?" His knees had been knocking, standing in the same office in which he now sat as an adult. At the time, the room had seemed three times larger and scary as any nightmare.

"You know what I mean, boy. Who was your father?"

"A bum who left my mother and me when I was seven years old, sir." His voice was firm. He was only fifteen years old, but he knew the score.

"Honest, at least. So you're the stepson of Max Kendrick. Why didn't you take his name?"

"I haven't earned it, sir. Besides, I'd like for my name to mean something, even if it was my father's name first." He'd thought at the time that a spark of respect had shone in Mac's eyes. Respect or not, when Madaline announced just before high school graduation that she and JT were going to be married, her father had flatly refused.

"JT, you know I've come to like you very much. You're a smart boy and a hard worker. I can't pretend you haven't impressed me. I think you have a bright future. But I can't abide my daughter marrying anybody, not you or the Duke of Cambridge, at such a young age. You have to understand that."

He had. Madaline had not. She'd thrown a fit, railing against her father. When JT had tried to calm her, she'd turned on him, too. Eventually, he and his Madaline had their way. But not for long. She was gone before their second anniversary.

Mac had stepped up in a big way. He'd taken JT under his wing and taught him everything he knew about business, including the sort of things you couldn't learn from a textbook. How to finesse. How to play both sides of the fence without either side ever being the wiser. How to leverage existing power to work a deal to your liking. It was like a-crash-course MBA training.

JT owed Mac everything. Still, years had passed since those early days. Over time, he'd taken on greater responsibility until he headed up the entire company. That experience had to count for something.

It all came down to how he handled this takeover attempt. He had to find out who was trying to buy out the company. Who in the world had that sort of money? Not many people.

The phone rang. JT was startled out of his dark reverie.
Who was calling his private line? "Hello?"

"Big brother."

His eyes widened. *Her*. He'd forgotten all about Veronica.
"Ronnie. Where are you?"

"At the moment, I'm in LA. But I'm sick to death of it. It's
disgusting. I thought it was high time I pay you a visit."

"Sure. It's only been ten years, Ron." "I've been busy."

"So my private investigator told me," he said. "Why
couldn't you be the one to tell me, instead?" "Oh, JT, you
know how it is," she said breezily.

"No, I don't. Why don't you tell me?" "Now's not the
time, sweetheart."

"Speaking of now not being the time," he said, thinking
fast, "now might not be the best time for you to come
back to town. Hear me out. Mac had a stroke a few nights

ago."

"Oh, no!" She sounded genuinely stricken. JT remembered how well the two of them had gotten along when she stayed here after his wedding to Becca. Of course they had. They were two peas in a pod, each trying to outdo the other regarding outrageous stories that would make a sailor blush.

"So you understand," he continued, "why now isn't the best time for a visit."

"I disagree. I think this is the best time. I'm sure poor little Maddie's upset over her grandpa."

Something about her tone of voice irritated JT more than he could say. As though she cared. "Don't talk about Maddie like you know her. She's almost eighteen years old. She's not a little girl anymore. Though, you're right —she's devastated over Mac's stroke. You're the last person she needs to see right now. A virtual stranger."

"Ouch, big brother. Somebody got out of bed on the wrong side this morning." He closed his eyes, forcing himself to count to ten. She got under his skin like nobody else could. The beauty of little sisters.

"It's been a tense time all around," he admitted, calmer now. "I mean what I say. Now's not the time. Give us a few weeks, at least. We should know by then whether Mac will pull through this, and how well. Then you can come and stay as long as you like."

"That works for me. I have some friends in Denver I'd like to visit, anyway. I could hit them up for a while."

He wanted to ask whether she had a place to live or if she planned on being a nomad for the rest of her life, then thought better of it. He wasn't sure he wanted to know, even if he had the time or patience to listen to her excuses.

They made arrangements for her to reach out to him in three weeks. "We're throwing Maddie's birthday party around that time. Maybe you could make it out for that." He had no intention of inviting her, envisioning the blow-up that would result. If he didn't mention it, though, she'd be hurt and accuse him of trying to sweep her under the rug.

"Sounds great. I'll give you a call in three weeks, then. I'd have you call me, but I don't know where I'll be. Ta!" She hung up. As always, it felt like a tornado had passed over him.

She hadn't had an easy life, he remembered. She'd been only three years old when their father left. She had no memory of him. Daddy issues had plagued her throughout her adolescence. She'd become way too attached to their stepfather—almost obsessive. When their parents had broached the idea of boarding school, she'd threatened to kill herself. JT had known she would never try anything like that. It was just her overly-dramatic personality. If she'd been running around Europe, rubbing elbows with royalty, he could imagine her tendencies were even more theatrical.

His line ran again. Would it ever end? He looked at the ID, recognizing the number this time. "Pressley." His voice was warm, intimate.

"Are you ever coming back?" She sounded sexy, with that throaty voice that drove him wild. There was something else beneath it, though. A plea.

"Of course ͵I am," he said. "There's a lot going on here, as you know. We're at the hospital nearly all the time, meeting with doctors. I have my daughter to consider, too. She's a wreck."

"Poor thing," Pressley crooned. "It's just that I miss you, so much. I miss your body. I miss your scent. Everything about you."

The need in her voice reached through the phone, straight to his manhood. He stirred.

"Where are you right now?" he asked. "In your office. With the door closed."

"What are you wearing?" He leaned back in his chair, stroking himself through his pants. Something about her voice always did it for him.

"The little black pinstripe suit. You know the one. You love the way my butt looks when I wear it." "What are you wearing underneath?"

"The red lace bra and panties you bought for me. With the

garter belt, and stockings with seams up the back. I know how much you love that, too." JT closed his eyes, imagining her luscious, curvy body in the get-up she'd just described. He ached, throbbing almost painfully.

"Don't you want to see me like this? Touch my body? Make me scream your name?" she asked, her voice deep and intimate.

"I do," he breathed.

"You can have me. Whenever, however. You know that."

His willpower broke. "What are you doing tonight?" he asked. "Anything you want," she replied almost instantly.

"Meet me at the Four Seasons. Ten o'clock. You know the name." They'd spent many nights there, and the occasional nooner when his office just wouldn't do.

"I can't wait. I've missed you so much."

"Me, too." He hung up, wishing there was a way he could get himself to stop this affair. There was no way it would end well.

Chapter 24

"Grandpa Mac. Can you hear me?"

Maddie was sitting by Mac's bedside. Ever since they'd brought him home from the hospital, she'd spent most of her time in a chair beside the bed. She couldn't leave him. What if he needed her for something? Her father reminded her of the excellent nursing staff staying at the house around the clock, but it meant nothing. They weren't the same as having family with him.

Mac opened his eyes and smiled at her. She smiled back. He looked much better than he had three weeks earlier, right after the stroke. She'd never been more scared in her life. When the first stroke hit, she was too little to understand. The grownups only told her Grandpa Mac was sick, and she'd thought that meant he had a cold.

This time, when she saw her father and William lifting him off the floor of his room, she'd honestly thought he was dead. He'd looked dead, at least. Becca had gripped her arm tightly, when she came in and saw his condition. Maddie had been too distraught to notice. She'd thought Becca was trying to hold her back from rushing to him.

"Grandpa, do you have the energy?" He nodded emphatically, so Maddie brought out the board. It was something she'd made up when he first came home a week earlier, a piece of foam board with words written on it in marker. Common words, like *yes, no, thirsty, hungry, tired, maybe, what is it, why, I see.* And, of course, *I love you.*

As soon as she brought out the board and held it in front of him, Grandpa pointed at that phrase. "I love you, too," she said, kissing his cheek.

What is it, he said.

She sighed heavily. "Grandpa, I've been doing a lot of thinking. I don't want to leave for school in three weeks."

No, he said. He pointed again and again. "Let me explain."

No. He glared at her.

"It's not only because of you," she said. "I was already thinking about postponing my first semester way before you had the stroke. I swear. I told my friend ̗Suzie, all about it before you even got sick."

Why?

"Because…I didn't want to leave you and Daddy alone." He looked at her, frowning.

Why?

"You know why."

No.

"Becca."

I see. He sighed. *Why?*

"I don't trust her, and I know you don't, either. So don't bother telling me you do." He smiled ever so slightly. "Yes. I know."

Why? Then he pointed to Maddie.

"Why me? Why don't I?" He nodded. She didn't want to tell him what she'd seen on the coroner's report—no sense getting him worked up. Instead, she said, "I never felt like she wanted to be here. A part of the family, I mean. She doesn't care. She just…"

What is it?

"She just wanted Daddy's money. Your money." A heavy sigh. *Yes.*

"What happens when I'm not here to protect you from her?"

He shook his head. It seemed as though he was almost

laughing. *No.*

"Maybe she's only been nice to you because I'm here ,—and she knows I wouldn't let her get away with being mean to you?"

He seemed to be thinking this over. *Maybe.*

"See? What if she's mean to you when nobody else is around? What if she hurts you?" There was nothing on the board for this, of course. He looked her in the eye and shrugged.

"That's it? A shrug? Like it doesn't matter?"

Yes.

Her eyes filled with tears. "I can't accept that, Grandpa. I love you too much."

I love you.

"I know." She was about to put the board away when his gnarled hand clamped over her arm. He was struggling.

"Are you all right? Oh, my God." She was just about to call for the nurse, but he shook his head violently. He was still struggling. She realized he was trying to speak.

"Your…life…" he sputtered, forcing the words out.

"My life?" He nodded hard, falling against the pillows. It had wiped him out, leaving him panting for breath. Tears filled her eyes. She smoothed his hair from his forehead.

"You're my life," she whispered.

Chapter 25

Maddie took a walk, thinking about what Grandpa Mac had tried to tell her. It was her life to live. She knew that. She had to build something for herself.

What was so bad about putting that on hold for now?

Her feet took her in the direction of the cottage Elix called home. He'd been living on the grounds for over three years. They'd been somewhat acquainted before then, running in the same circles, but he was four years older than her. When you were a teenager, four years feels like a lifetime.

Maddie remembered what she thought of him back in the day, before she knew him as well as she did now. He was handsome—extremely so. She'd even had a little crush on him back then, a silly schoolgirl thing. His olive skin, that thick dark hair, the dark eyes she'd thought were so mysterious. He had a ready smile, too, which had endeared him to her even more. Just a flash of that white smile had been enough to make her knees go weak.

But she was only fourteen back then. A freshman in high school when he'd been a senior. He was the star of the football team, a talented quarterback. Everybody's favorite person. The girls were all crazy about him. He was a sure bet for a full ride to any school he chose—they were clamoring over him.

Maddie knocked on the door to his cottage, wondering if he was even at home. The door opened. "Hey. What's up?" She saw books spread out over his little kitchen table.

"Oh, you're studying. Of course, that was dumb. I forgot. I should go." She backed away, intending to leave.

"No, please. Stay. It's okay, I need a break, anyway." He

opened the door wider. She stepped inside.

The cottage was cute, homey. More than enough room for one person. It had housed caretakers for decades, ever since Mac bought the property and had the big house built.

"What's up? You look kind of upset." He sat in front of her at the kitchen table.

"I was just talking with Grandpa. Well, not talking, per se. You know what I mean."

"How's he doing?"

"He actually said two words tonight." Elix beamed. "That's great! What did he say?"

She took a deep breath, knowing he'd need context. "Your life." "Your life? What's that mean?"

"It means I don't want to go to college this semester." "No!" He looked stern.

"Exactly what he said," she replied sourly.

"Good. You need somebody else to help you get your head screwed on straight. Maddie, that's not a good idea. Get out of here. Go see more of the world. I've said it before: there's more to life than this place."

"I know you're right. But what about him? He needs me."

"Ah, I see. Your life. He's right. It *is* your life. You can't live it for him." "But he needs me, Elix."

"He has nurses. Doctors. A whole staff up there, just waiting to help him."

"That's not what I mean. It's all too much to explain." Maddie surprised herself by bursting into tears.

"Maddie!" Elix knelt beside her, wrapping his arms around her. She leaned against him. "I know it's been a lot lately, with Mac being sick. He and my grandfather were good friends. I like him a lot. I know you love him, but, and I hate to say this because I know how it sounds, that might be exactly why you need to go away. This might be perfect timing."

"How can you say that?" She sat up, wiping her eyes. "That's cruel."

"I didn't mean to be cruel. I'm only trying to think of you, the way your grandfather is." "But…it's not like I'm going to be able to focus on my work."

"That's your choice. I mean, I work my butt off all day out on the grounds, then I go to school at night and study when all I want to do is pass out, face-first on my bed. It's my choice whether or not I do that. See what I mean? I could use fatigue as an excuse…"

"Oh, you think I'm using an excuse?"

"No, that's just a word I used in my case. I could use fatigue as an excuse to avoid work, but that's not the choice I make. I choose to study. Even though I'm tired."

"Bravo," she said, sarcastic.

"Why did you even come here if all you were going to do was fight with me?"

Her shoulders slumped. "I'm sorry. You're right. You're the only person I could imagine coming to, and here I am, picking a fight."

"You want something to drink?" He got up, turning to the fridge.

"Just some water. I could use it." He handed her a bottle, which she held to her hot, tear-stained cheeks.

"Are you afraid of starting school?" Elix asked, and she knew he was carefully avoiding her eyes. "No! Not at all."

"It's just you never seemed very excited about it," he pointed out. She shrugged. "Maybe I'm not."

"I wish I were in your shoes. I'd trade places with you in a heartbeat." He leaned toward her. "Don't you see? You have a chance to make something of yourself. Your father can afford to send you literally anywhere. You're smart enough to score admission to, what? A half dozen Ivy League schools? Don't throw that away. Your grandfather will recover."

"What if he doesn't?" Maddie's voice was fretful.

"Then he doesn't. But either way, you'll be alive. See what I mean?" There was no cruelty in his voice. Maddie understood his point. He added, "I know he'd want you to take advantage of every chance to have a good life. Just like I do."

She smiled. "You do?"

He nodded. "I'm sure it's not easy for him to let you go. But when you love somebody, you want what's best for them. Even if it sucks for you."

Maddie didn't stay for much longer, not wanting to hold up his work. She walked back to the big house, the moonlight guiding her. She'd know the way in the pitch dark, of course. She'd walked it so many times over the past three years.

There was no denying the way it felt when Elix had wrapped her in his arms. She'd very easily leaned against him, hadn't she? And hadn't it felt good—too good?

She was no blushing virgin. Far from it. She'd dated a half dozen guys throughout high school, hooked up with a half dozen more. She'd never thought of it as a big deal. Sex was something kids in her world just did. They were all very mature, too mature for their age. Jaded from birth.

She'd never felt nearly the level of tension with them that she felt with Elix, and all he'd done was hold her while she cried. It was the same way when he helped her over the fence, that day weeks ago. She hadn't thought about it much at the time—she'd made herself forget about it—but now she remembered how it felt when he held her. It was so simple. Nothing sexy. But the sexiest she'd ever felt.

When you love somebody, you want what's best for them. Was he trying to tell her something?

Chapter 26

The last several days had been a whirlwind. Becca had been on the phone with caterers, musicians, rental companies, lighting vendors, valets, and more. She was exhausted—and now she had to look absolutely flawless for the party.

She was just getting back from the salon, where Iris had done wonders as always. Becca had described her dress— a white column dress with one exposed shoulder. Very simple, very chic. Iris had gone with a goddess-style hairdo, swept back and up with curls hanging down.

Many of the vendors were already present, the party planner Becca had hired for that day directing people here and there. It had been important to Becca that she did the bulk of the planning herself. She could easily have hired a planner to handle the entire event, but again, all that mattered was the impression that she was willing to work day and night for her stepdaughter's happiness. No party planner would do as good a job for her little girl as she would.

Becca gagged a little whenever she thought about it.

She hurried to her room, where she planned to dress and do her makeup. Along the way, she passed

Mac's room. The door was open. She would have walked straight past—no need to worry herself about that old buzzard today—but the sound of Maddie's quiet voice made her stop. She hovered just outside the door, out of sight of those inside the bedroom.

"I don't know, Grandpa," Maddie was fretting. "I'm still worried." Mac's speech had gotten slightly better. "Have…fun…"

"I'm going to try to, but it's hard with all that's on my mind. I mean, how can I stand there next to that woman and pretend we're one, big, happy family?"

"Have…to try…"

"I know I have to try. If only for Daddy's sake. I know it will make him happy." "It…will."

"Only…Grandpa, I hadn't told you this before because I didn't want to upset you. But I found out something about Becca that I think you should know."

"Mrs. Rossi?" Becca whirled around, one of their household staff having found her in the hall. She held a finger to her lips, hurrying toward the woman.

Just then, Maddie appeared at the door to Mac's room. "She's not home, Teresa."

"Yes, I am, dear. I just came in." She smiled at Maddie from the other end of the hall. "What do you think of my hair?"

"It's pretty," Maddie said, smiling. "It'll go great with your dress."

"I thought so, too." Becca turned to the housekeeper to find out the planner was looking for her. She dashed downstairs to find her, her mind in a whirl.

What the hell had that little brat been on the verge of saying? Perfect time for Teresa to come looking. She'd been so close to hearing what Maddie thought she knew.

After getting things settled about the placement of flowers around the room, Becca went back upstairs. This time, Mac's door was closed. She listened closely for any sounds of conversation but heard nothing. Had Maddie gone back to her story?

What could that story have been?

Becca went to her bedroom, closing the door behind her. She could have thrown something, she was so anxious. Her entire body crackled with nervous tension. She paced back and forth across the luxurious room, going through her memory to find any hint of a story Maddie would know about and find necessary to share with Mac.

It was possible, of course, that one of Becca's so-called friends had blabbed in front of one of their kids the secrets of Becca's misdoings. That kid, whoever they were, could have told Maddie. Maybe she'd found out about Becca's affair with the pool boy or the fling with the college student they'd brought in to help Maddie with her French lessons. That would make sense.

No, it wouldn't. Hadn't she heard Maddie talk about being worried? There wasn't much to worry about if all she knew was that her stepmother had had an affair. She was a big girl. She knew how the world worked. Becca thought she'd been around the block a few times too many for a girl her age, in fact.

What could it be, then? *Wait. No. It couldn't be. Could it?*

Becca hated the way she fled to the secret stash of vodka she kept in her closet. She pulled out the bottle, not bothering to find a glass. She poured the liquid down her throat, trying desperately to calm herself.

There was no way Maddie knew about Frank. How could she? Yet it was the only thing Becca had ever done which could truly warrant the concern she heard in Maddie's voice. Otherwise, all she had were plans. Plans she'd never shared with a single person.

Had Becca ever so much as hinted at the true nature of Frank's death? No. She wasn't stupid. She'd worked for an entire year on that by slowly feeding the man cyanide, just enough so it wouldn't be obvious but enough to kill him over time. It had taken all the patience she could muster to wait it out. He'd slowly wasted away, never understanding why. She'd counted on his aversion to doctors too, knowing he'd only go if something really serious happened. Coughing up blood, that sort of thing.

So she gave him just barely enough to make a difference. Eventually, her patience had paid off. She'd received ten million dollars.

She would put nothing past Maddie when it came to digging up dirt on her. Another swig from the bottle. With everything a person could dig up on the internet nowadays? What if she got her hands on the death certificate or the coroner's report? Stranger things had happened. Maddie was a smart girl. She wasn't one to let go of an idea once it occurred to her. If she'd suspected Becca of killing her first husband, she would have done whatever it took to find out for sure.

This was a nightmare.

Slow down, Rebecca Jean. You don't know anything for sure. She took another drink, this one better than the other two. She was starting to calm down, just as she always did after visiting her vodka bottle. There were times when her increasing dependence on alcohol was a worry. Now was not one of those times; she could only be relieved by its presence.

All right. No sense in getting any more worked up tonight. There was no telling what the little brat knew. She'd have to get to the bottom of it, somehow, but this wasn't the time. Becca reminded herself to be calm, tackle what had to be tackled tonight, and then worry about the rest tomorrow.

***

An hour later, JT came in, still dressed in the suit he wore to work that day.

"You men," Becca chided jokingly. "All you have to do is shower, shave, and dress. It's so easy for you."

"Nobody says you have to spend all day getting ready for a party," JT reminded her. He came up behind her where she sat at her vanity, and kissed the back of her neck. "Besides, you don't need to.

You look just beautiful to me with no makeup at all."

The funny thing was, she knew he meant it. He didn't give out false compliments. It was moments like this when her heart softened toward him.

"Thank you. For the record, you look nice without makeup, too." He laughed, stripping down as he headed for the in-suite bathroom they shared.

Little did he know that it took her three tries to get her makeup right. By the time she'd gotten started, her hands wouldn't seem to do what she had wanted them to do.

She'd looked like a clown.

The wastebasket by her feet was full of cold cream-stained tissues and an empty vodka bottle.

She didn't want to attempt putting her dress on by herself, for fear of getting makeup all over the delicate white fabric. She had an idea.

"Maddie?" Becca knocked softly on the bedroom door. "Are you decent?"

"Yeah, come in." Becca stepped into the room and was unable to stifle a genuine gasp at her stepdaughter's transformation.

"Maddie, you are really beautiful." She was wearing a pink taffeta A-line dress with a bow at one hip. It was sleeveless, the bodice cut in a wide V-shape. Her long, dark hair was back in a modest chignon.

"Thank you," Maddie said with a slight smile.

"I was wondering if you could help me with my dress."

She'd brought it with her, draped over one arm. "I'd have your father do it but, well, you know how men are." She giggled.

Maddie giggled, too. "All thumbs," she agreed.

"Exactly, and the last thing I need is to get makeup on this thing. Can you imagine?" She grimaced, and they laughed again.

Becca removed her robe, then held a hand towel in front of her face as Maddie lowered the dress over her head.

"Are you ready for tonight?" Becca asked.

"I guess so. I'm a little nervous," Maddie admitted. "Why?"

"I don't know. Did you ever just get a bad feeling about something? Like a gut feeling?"

"You have a gut feeling about tonight?" Becca mulled this over. Was that what she wanted to share with Mac? That she felt forced into having this party even though she didn't want it? No, that couldn't be it—besides, she was the one who'd wanted it in the first place. Becca had only agreed to throw it.

"I don't know. It sounds silly." "Not so silly."

Maddie bit her lip. "I invited someone who I really wanted to come, but I don't think they're coming."

"Did they RSVP?" "No, never."

"How rude." The dress was on now, and Becca slid her arm through the single armhole. She turned to look at herself in the mirror. Perfect.

"Yeah. I hand-delivered the invite and everything."

"Who are you talking about?" Becca turned to her, intrigued now. "Oh. Um, Elix."

"Elix? And he couldn't even come up to the house to let you know whether or not he wanted to come? That doesn't sound like him." Hmm. So Maddie had a thing for the stable boy, huh? Becca couldn't blame her. He was gorgeous.

"No, it's not like him at all. I'm wondering why he couldn't just say no." Maddie bit her lip, looking out the window in the direction of the cottage in which Elix lived.

"Maybe it's not easy for him," Becca offered. "After all, this life…it's not the place for him anymore." Maddie turned to her, anger on her face. "Now, now, don't take it out on me. He made his choices. I'm sure it's not easy, feeling like an outsider now. That's all I meant."

Maddie turned to the window. "Yeah. I just…wish he knew I didn't feel like he's an outsider."

She was in love with him. Very interesting. Becca went to her, patting her on the shoulder. "There, there. Try to have a good time tonight. You can always talk to him tomorrow. Give him hell.

Sometimes a man needs a woman to give him a little hell." She winked. Maddie laughed. It was probably the first time they'd had a pleasant conversation. It must have been the vodka.

"I have to finish getting ready." Becca turned, picking up her robe.

"Becca?" She turned, looking back at Maddie. "In case I forget to say it later, thanks for tonight."

"You're welcome." She smiled again, leaving the room. The smile melted the moment she stepped into the hall. Hopefully that warmed things up enough between them that Maddie wouldn't go running to her father tonight. Now it was just a matter of finding out if she'd said anything to Mac, but how would she do that? He wouldn't tell her, either way. He hated her.

There was only one thing she could do. Becca looked at his closed bedroom door. Did she have it in her to take care of yet another man who stood in her way?

"Becca." JT was standing in the doorway to their room, beckoning her. "I have something for you." In their room, he presented her with a long, velvet box. She beamed at him and opened it.

"Oh, JT, honey." A diamond and platinum necklace. It

would complement her dress perfectly. "You're too generous."

"No such thing," he said, stepping behind her to fasten the clasp. She admired herself in the mirror.

"Now you look like the goddess you truly are," he murmured, kissing her shoulder. She smiled, unable to help wondering how much longer this would last if her secret ever got out.

Chapter 27

Maddie stood by her bedroom window, looking out over the grounds. Cars were beginning to stream down the driveway; the hired valets opened doors, greeted guests, and then drove the cars to a makeshift parking lot on the other side of the property. Members of their staff shuttled the attendants back in golf carts rented for the occasion. It was quite a production. And all for her.

Why wasn't she happy about it? One word: Elix.

With everything on her mind, Elix was the one person who kept popping to the surface of her thoughts. She was unhappy, remembering the last time she saw him. They hadn't parted on the best of terms.

It had been a week since she walked down to the cottage to check on him. He'd been standoffish, always too busy to talk when she visited him at the stables. One of the mares was about to foal, another was sick. He'd had his hands full. After days of this she decided to go straight to him and ask if she'd said or done something to tick him off.

He'd been civil toward her when he opened the door, asking her to have a seat before turning his back to her. She'd known there was something wrong, then.

"What's with you?" she asked, watching his back as he washed the few dishes in the little sink.

"Nothing. What's with you?"

"I'm not the one giving anybody the cold shoulder," she said. "Sorry. I'm just tired. It's been a long week."

"Is that it?"

"I said it was, didn't I?" His tone was sharp. He still hadn't turned around. "You don't sound convincing."

"Sorry I didn't fall on my knees as soon as you walked in, Princess."

"Would you knock it off, or tell me what the problem is? Either way. I don't have to sit here and take this." She'd stood, going to the door.

"Don't go," he'd said, turning to her. "I don't mean to be a pain. You didn't do anything." Maddie hesitated. He smiled to reassure her.

"Okay." She'd returned to the couch.

"Tell me about the party plans. How's everything coming along?"

"Ugh." Elix had already been filled in on the drama she'd been going through with Becca. "That woman is making me crazy. I know this isn't about me. It's all about her. I don't even want the stupid party. Not when Grandpa Mac is upstairs, sick. It doesn't feel right."

"It's a gesture," Elix had reminded her. "And a way for the family to remind people you're still strong, even if your grandfather is sick."

"How are you so smart about things like this? You always have this other point of view I hadn't thought about. You make me feel like an idiot."

"Because you are an idiot."

"Thanks. So yeah, that's what it is. A big old mess. Daddy's all excited because Senator Marlowe's coming. As if I cared. I'm supposed to be honored. All I want to do is have a little fun with my friends. But no, we have to hire a string orchestra and twenty parking attendants and a bunch of other crap I don't care about."

"I wish I could be there to see it," Elix mumbled.

"Wait, what?" He'd still been standing at the sink with his back turned. She couldn't see his face. "What did you say?"

"I said, I wish I could be there to see it." "What do you

mean? Where will you be?" "Here, I guess. Where else would I be?"

"Hang on." Maddie had jumped from the couch, going to him. She'd turned him to face her. "You'd be at my party. Like I thought you would be."

"You thought I would be?" "Of course!"

"Then why wasn't I invited?"

Maddie had gasped, stepping back. "Is that what this is all about? Why you've been ignoring me all week? You thought you weren't invited?"

"Usually an invitation means a person's invited to a party. I didn't get an invitation."

"Oh, Elix…" *That Becca.* "I had you on my list. I guess it was just a mix-up. Of course ⸗I want you to be there! Are you kidding?"

He hadn't been convinced. His eyes were narrowed. "You sure about that?" "Sure I'm sure! Jeez. You're my best friend, you idiot!"

He'd laughed. "You don't think it'll be weird, my being there?"

"What do I care about weird? You're the best person I know. You'd better be there." She'd smiled, punching him playfully on the arm. She hadn't been smiling on the inside, though. On the inside she'd been cursing her stepmother for interfering yet again.

"Come on," Maddie had offered. "Let's go up to the pool and have a swim. It's the perfect night for it."

"You think so? We won't piss anybody off? I mean, Maddie…I'm glad you see me as a friend. I see you that way, too, but I work here. I'm not…you."

"I don't care about that. And besides, you're the only person who sees you that way. Everybody else thinks of you as family." She'd beamed at him and had honestly meant it.

They'd walked back to the big house, talking the whole

time. Now that the discomfort around the party had been cleared up, Maddie had felt at ease venting her frustration over the way the party had blown up.

"Do you have a tuxedo?" she'd asked.

"Yeah, somewhere. My grandfather made me get one for the parties we went to." "Good. It's formal dress."

"Ugh. What a drag."

"I know! I wanted something casual and fun. Not some stuffy black tie event. It's my party in name only, I swear."

"At least you'll get a ton of gifts. Everyone will be trying to outdo each other, so your dad will like them the best."

"Isn't it pathetic?" She'd laughed, thinking how stupid grownups were. Acting like kids, pretending to be sophisticated, but really fighting each other for attention from the coolest kid in school.

"It's really a big deal for Becca, isn't it?" Elix had asked.

"Yeah. You'd think it was her birthday instead of mine."
Maddie had been fuming. "Will there even be music?"

"Oh, that's the best part! Some boring string orchestra. Can
you imagine?" "Save me a dance." He'd said it so softly
she'd barely made out the words.

"I'll save you every dance," she'd replied. And she'd
meant it, with all her heart. There was nobody she'd rather
spend the party with than him.

Elix had stopped walking, Maddie turning to him. They
were standing beside the house just beyond the patio and
pool. He had moved toward her, slowly. Maddie had never
before seen the look that was in his eye.

Her heart had pounded in her chest, her body trembling
despite the warmth in the air. Was he going to kiss her?
Did she even want him to?

The lights around the patio switched on, all at once,
flooding the area with a bright glare. She and Elix and
covered their eyes against the harshness.

Chapter 28

"Who's there?" Maddie's heart had sunk. That voice could only belong to one person. "It's us, Becca. Me and Elix." She'd thrown Elix a desperate glance. He'd grimaced.

"You and Elix? What are you doing out here at this time of night?" Becca had stumbled toward them, the heel of her slipper getting caught between two flagstones on the path from the house to patio. Maddie had wondered how much of that clumsiness had to do with the martini glass Becca had been holding.

"It's not that late. We were just hanging out." Maddie had walked to the patio, Elix following her.

"I don't think it's appropriate for the two of you to be walking around the grounds together at this time of night. Elix, it would be best for you to go back to the cottage. Don't you have to get up early to start work?"

Maddie's hands had clenched. She'd wanted to rip Becca's blonde head off, or at least knock her into the pool. Her face had burned with shame for Elix's sake.

He was much cooler and calmer, always the leveler head. "You're right, Mrs. Rossi. I'll say goodnight now. See you later, Maddie."

"See you." Maddie couldn't look at him. She'd been too ashamed.

Of what, though? She stood at the window, looking out toward the cottage as her guests arrived. What had she felt ashamed of? Her stepmother? Yes, Becca was worth feeling ashamed of. She was so blatantly snobby, making sure he remembered he worked for them. Maddie knew he felt like he didn't measure up to the Rossis and the Henrys. But he did. His family was just as highly valued as theirs.

Chapter 29

Maddie had hand delivered an invitation straight to Elix's front door after finding out about Becca's 'accidental' oversight. He had never RSVP'd. In fact, she hadn't spoken to him since that night.

Why? What was so different now?

Was it the way she'd been sure he was going to kiss her before Becca interrupted? If he had, would Maddie have let him?

She leaned against the window frame, staring off into the gathering darkness of the summer sky. Yes. She would have. She'd have wrapped her arms around his neck and kissed him for all she was worth. She'd been wanting to do it for years. Ever since the day she met him, when she was a lowly freshman and he was the star quarterback.

Maybe he was thinking better of his impulse now. It was easy to get carried away in the heat of the moment. A night swim. Two young people, hormones raging all over the place. Now that he'd had time to think it over, he was probably regretting it.

Either that or he still didn't think he was good enough. If Maddie didn't know her father would kill her for it, she'd run straight down to the cottage to tell him how good she thought he was. He was noble and wise. He worked harder than anybody she knew, breaking his back to make up for his mistakes. He was worth ten of any other boy she knew.

A knock at the door. "Maddie?" It was Suzie and Jenna, squealing with excitement.

"Come in." They were the last people she wanted to see right now.

"Maddie, what's wrong?" She'd tried to put on a happy face for their sake. It clearly hadn't worked, judging from their reactions.

"Nothing. Just tired. Now I have to go down and face all those people."

"Here." Jenna reached into her little clutch, pulling out a pill box. "Caffeine pills. They'll perk you right up."

"Got anything stronger?" she joked.

"Wow, you are in a bad mood. I have some Percocet, too, if you want that."

"Nah, I'm only kidding. You know I don't go in for that." Maddie never asked where her friend always managed to get her hands on meds, and Jenna had never offered her secret.

"It's caffeine, Maddie. You drink coffee, right?" Jenna smirked. Maddie shook her head. "I'll be fine without it."

"I'll take the Perc, if you don't mind." Suzie took one of

the larger tablets, washing it down with the mini flask in her own purse. Maddie took a swig of the booze, then went to her bathroom to rinse out the booze with mouthwash. All she needed was for her father to smell bourbon on her breath.

The two girls joined her, primping before heading down the party. Maddie looked at them in a new light. Kids ; pretending to be grownups. Old before their time. She knew it was something Elix would have said. Why was she thinking his thoughts?

"Come on," Maddie said brightly, linking arms with her best girlfriends. "Let's go down and have some fun. Maybe I can convince my dad to let us have one little drink." She was determined to have some fun and push away her dark thoughts. She could worry about Elix and her family tomorrow.

Chapter 30

"Beautiful Maddie."

Maddie felt a sick sensation in her stomach. She knew that voice. Only one person in the world managed to sound so nauseatingly perverted while saying nice things.

"Bobby." She said his name before even turning around, certain he was who she'd find. Sure enough, there he was. Standing roughly four inches from her. She took a step back.

"It's nice to see you. I'm sure my father's happy your family could make it," Maddie said, smiling. Her eyes weren't smiling, though. They were searching the room, looking for a way out of this situation. He had her practically cornered against a wall. She'd been getting herself some punch when he found her.

"You look gorgeous tonight. Sexy. Grown up." He reached out to her, fingering the pink taffeta bow at her waist. It was all she could do to keep from swatting his hand away. The only thing stopping her was the relationship their fathers had. She knew Daddy wanted her to be nice to Bobby.

"Thanks," she muttered, feeling dirty. How did he manage to do that? Maybe it as the way he nearly drooled on himself when he said it. He was disgusting.

"Hey, Maddie. Who's your friend?" Suzie had sidled up to them. *Oh, thank God*, Maddie thought.

"Suze, this is Bobby Marlowe. Senator Marlowe's son. Bobby, this is my friend Suzie Grant." "Suzie." He looked disinterested in Suzie, his eyes going right back to Maddie.

"Hey, Suze, come to the powder room with me. I, uh, need

help with something." She took Suzie by the hand and slid past the oh-so-close Bobby, hurrying away.

"What are you doing?" Suzie hissed as Maddie pulled her along. "He's gorgeous, and the Senator's son!"

"Yeah, yeah," Maddie said, breathless and grim. "I know all that. He's also a creep." Then a bunch of their friends walked through the door leading from the hall, erasing the strain from Maddie's mind. If they hadn't come in at just that moment, she might have had the chance to tell her friend what Bobby Marlowe was all about.

*****

JT was deep in conversation with one of his executives when Becca entered the room. A light smattering of applause rose from the guests closest to the door as she did.

He could see why. She was radiant, glowing. He crossed the room, a smile on his face. "You're exquisite," he murmured, kissing her cheek. She smiled, even blushed slightly.

"Thank you," she whispered, her hand gently touching the necklace he'd given her. He smiled in acknowledgment.

"So," he said, turning to the room. "I'd say this is already a success."

"She deserves it," Becca gushed. He agreed. Nobody deserved this more than his daughter.

Chapter 31

Becca smiled through her disgust. Her foot, Maddie deserved it. She deserved none of this. Becca could only hope the night turned out well and that everyone remembered her as the benevolent, beautiful stepmother who only wanted her little family to be happy. All the while she'd be eating her heart out, wondering what Maddie had on her.

"I see the Marlowes are here," Becca said, waving to Stephen and Bethany. JT led her to them.

"JT, you're the second luckiest man in the world," Stephen

said, kissing Becca's cheek. "Next to me, of course."

"Always a flatterer. You're such a politician," Becca laughed, turning from him to give his wife an air kiss.

"Did this husband of yours tell you we might be in business together soon?" Stephen asked. Becca turned to JT just in time to see him flash a look of warning his friend's way.

"You know JT keeps all that deep, dark business stuff to himself, Senator," Becca demurred. They laughed together while Becca made a mental note to ask her husband about this at a later time. There had to be a reason he hadn't mentioned it to her —and why he looked irritated at the topic being broached in the first place. It wasn't like him to keep things from her.

There was a string orchestra playing at the far end of the room, and Stephen took his wife by the hand for a dance. Becca smiled at them as they took to the floor.

"Not a word," JT warned, looking around the room.

"I didn't say anything," Becca replied through her teeth, still smiling. Not looking at him. "I'll tell you about it later."

"I wasn't even going to ask, sweetheart." She reached over to wipe a smudge of lipstick from his cheek. Then she turned away, intending to walk off and greet Lauralee and her husband.

"By the way, I've been meaning to tell you for weeks but keep getting distracted," JT added, catching her by the elbow. "Veronica's coming back to town." The smug glee was clear in his voice.

Becca turned to him, eyes wide. *Her.*

They'd have a lot to talk about in the morning.

Chapter 32

Maddie was trying to enjoy the party. She reminded herself more than once to pay attention to the conversation guests were trying to have with her. She didn't want to be rude; she wanted to have fun. All she could do was think about her grandfather…and look for Elix.

She knew him. He was too proud to show his face, but that didn't stop her from hoping he'd change his mind and come up to the house. Every time a new guest arrived, her eyes would go to the door. Hoping against hope he'd walk in, dressed in a tuxedo, looking more handsome than any other man in the room. No such luck, however. The party had been going for two hours and still no sign of him.

She stepped outside to get a breath of fresh air. Though it was much cooler inside, it was becoming stuffy with all the people mingling around, especially now that the dancing had picked up.

Maddie felt a chill, despite the warmth in the air. She crossed her arms, shivering. "Cold?"

She spun, finding Elix standing only feet from her. Dressed in a tee and jeans.

"What are you doing? Those aren't party clothes." She heard the disappointment in her voice even though she was relieved to see him at all.

"I'm not here for the party." "Why *are* you here, then?"

"I came to see you. Just to see you. I didn't expect you to come out, though I'm glad you did."

"Lurking around outside my party? That's weird. That's

not like you." It was all she could think to say. It wasn't easy to process his words. It sounded like he was trying to tell her something she wasn't ready to hear.

"You're right. That's not like me. I've been wondering what the hell's wrong with me for a long time."

She stood, just looking at him. "What do you think it is?" she asked, still at a loss.

He was quiet for a long time, staring at the ground. He took a deep breath. Maddie was holding hers, waiting to hear what he would say.

"I don't know," he mumbled, he looked up from under his long dark lashes and took a step toward her.

He stopped right in front of her. She could smell the scent of fresh soap on his skin. She looked up into his dark eyes as she tilted her head up toward him and closed her eyes. Elix gently ran his thumb across her bottom lip and then turned to leave.

"Elix!" It was a plea, straight from her heart. "Don't go."

"I have to." He jerked his head in the direction of the house. "It's clear you're the only person who thinks I belong here. You're one person against hundreds. I know you. You would spend your time at my side, just to be sure I wasn't alone. That wouldn't score any points."

"I don't care about points!" Maddie insisted.

"You should. You'll have to. That's how the world works. It's time to grow up. Your father? Your grandfather? It's great, the way they treat you. But not everybody is going to let you have your way just because it makes you happy. It's time to get over that." He turned, having gotten the last word. Maddie decided to run after him, no matter how it looked to leave her own birthday party.

"Maddie! Get in here! They want you to cut the cake!" Jenna and Suzie took her by the arms, pulling her back through the French doors. Elix had already disappeared, part of the shadows.

Chapter 33

Becca stood off to the side while her stepdaughter cut the absolutely ridiculous birthday cake JT had insisted on. There weren't many aspects of the planning process which got his attention, but this had been one of them. It looked like a wedding cake for Christ's sake, seven tiers, covered in white fondant and life-like pink sugar roses. *Anything to catch the eye*, Becca told herself. His baby deserved nothing but the very best. Bile nearly rose in her throat. Maddie raised the silver cake cutter, slicing into the bottom tier.

Three hundred guests, and nearly every one of them was

holding up a phone to record the cutting. Becca wondered if they realized how ridiculous they looked. What ever happened to observing a moment and letting it pass?

She looked across the table, to where the Marlowes stood. Stephen had his hand on Bobby's shoulder. There was a distinct likeness to the two men. Stephen was so youthful they could have passed for brothers. Becca could see Bobby would be just as handsome as his father when he reached that age.

There was something disturbing about him, though. She'd heard he got into trouble a while back, some strange accusations from a girl. Then there was the way Lauralee had given the Marlowes the cold shoulder when she first saw them earlier in the evening. Becca remembered her daughter had been interning with Stephen this summer. Had something happened? It occurred to her that Lauralee hadn't mentioned Evie in weeks, though they spoke on the phone nearly every day.

There was no denying the way Bobby was looking at Maddie, how his eyes followed her fingers when she raised them to her mouth, licking a bit of frosting off the tips. Maybe the brat had made a good point when she'd protested his invitation. There'd been no way to avoid it without insulting the Marlowes, even though he gave Becca the creeps.

Chapter 34

"Hey, Maddie." Suzie tapped Maddie on the shoulder.

"Excuse me," Maddie said to the woman who had pulled her aside to rave about how beautiful she looked. She'd called Maddie anorexic. A strange compliment, especially considering that Maddie was eating a piece of her birthday cake at the time. One of Becca's weird friends.

Maddie turned to Suzie. "What's up?"

"There's something I have to show you." She took Maddie by the hand, leading her away from the crowd and out through the French doors that led to the back patio.

"What are you doing? My father will kill me if he catches me messing around tonight. He already told me so."

"Don't worry about it. If he finds out about this, he'll be happy." Suzie giggled. Maddie wondered what the hell was up her friend's sleeve, whether she'd taken more than one Percocet tonight. Suzie let her around the side of the house, to the roundabout in the front.

"What's happening?" Maddie looked around. There was a single car parked there. She could just barely make out a figure seated behind the steering wheel.

"Come on! He's going to take us for a ride to get some really great stuff," Suzie said, pulling Maddie toward the car.

"What stuff? What are you talking about? Who is *he*?" Maddie asked. Suzie opened the passenger door, then turned.

"A friend of yours," she giggled. Before she could protest, Maddie was being shoved into the car. Suzie burst out laughing.

"Have fun, you two!" She waved, then ran back to the party.

Maddie looked to her left towards the man in the driver's seat. Her mouth fell open in horror. "Bobby!"

Chapter 35

"Where's Maddie?"

JT approached Becca, looking around the ballroom. Becca sighed. Wasn't it just like that little brat to run out on her own party, when they had strictly forbade it?

"I'll look for her, if you want. I could use a breath of fresh air. The Senator's motioning for you." Becca nodded her head in Stephen's direction.

"Don't be hard on her. Just bring her back." JT walked away.

"No, wouldn't want to be hard on her," Becca muttered to herself. "Wouldn't want to make her pay for her attitude." Or for the way she sneaked around behind everybody's back. The little brat thought she was so clever.

She stepped outside, the humid air a contrast from the cool comfort of the ballroom. Where was that girl? Leave it to her to disappear during a party held in her honor. If Maddie pulled some stunt that made her parents look like the bad guys tonight, Becca would lose her mind. She'd worked too hard for this night.

Chapter 36

"What's this all about?" Maddie asked, her heart hammering wildly. She pressed herself against the door as far from Bobby as she could get. Her hand searched for the handle, her eyes never leaving him.

"I've been trying to get some time alone with you ─all night long," he slurred. "Why have you been ducking me?"

"I'm—I'm sorry, Bobby. It's my party, you know? Everybody wants time with the birthday girl. I can't ignore everybody else. My dad would be mad at me."

"Wouldn't want to piss off Daddy." Bobby laughed. "Now we have some time to ourselves. I asked your friend to get you out here, so I could have some alone time with the birthday girl." He grinned, his intentions immediately clear.

"I don't know, Bobby," Maddie blubbered, close to tears. "I have to get back to the party. They're going to come looking for me. I'm going to be in big trouble if they can't find me."

"Believe me," he murmured, leaning toward her, "if they know you're with me, they won't be upset. Our dads are such good friends and all. They'll be glad we got together."

Terror swept through her as he moved closer.

Chapter 37

Becca walked around the side of the house, over the stone path. If she found that bitch screwing around with her friends, there'd be hell to pay.

There was a car in the turnaround. Strange. All the cars had been parked elsewhere on the grounds. She took a step closer.

"No! I said no, Bobby! Let me out!" Becca heard it through the closed windows of the car. She knew the voice, recognized the dress.

Instead of continuing to the car and demanding Maddie be

let out, she shrank back against the side of the house. Waiting to see where this went.

***

"What are you doing? Stop! I said stop!" Maddie fought him as hard as she could. She kicked, scratched, punched. Nothing made a bit of a difference. She might as well have been hitting a brick wall. He never registered any of it.

She screamed, praying somebody would hear her. All the staff were eating in the kitchen; the noise from the party was too loud for her to be heard.

Bobby reeked of alcohol, sweat. His hands were everywhere, his mouth nuzzling her neck, then her cleavage.

"You want this," he growled, his hands on her thighs now. He grabbed her panties, tearing them. Maddie screamed.

***

A scream.

Mac opened his eyes, his head turning toward the open window. Had he dreamt it? No, another scream. From who? A cold chill ran down his spine. Somehow, he knew it was Maddie.

He heard a car's engine turn over, then fade into the distance. He couldn't cry out for help. Trapped in his own body.

***

Bobby's car sped away, down the gravel drive. With Maddie screaming to be let out.

Becca stood in the shadows, watching as the taillights grew smaller. Eventually, they disappeared into the blackness.

She turned to go back inside, intent on rejoining the party. She could enjoy herself now.

Web Of Lies

Chapter 1

JT and Becca stood side-by-side, waving off the last of the guests. It was past two in the morning, and he was exhausted.

He was also furious. "Where the hell is that girl?"

Becca held up a hand. "Sweetheart, please. Don't get yourself all worked up, not at this late hour. You know you won't be able to get to sleep if you're too excited."

He turned and stormed into the house. "Her own party, and she can't be bothered to stick around until the end! I never saw her after she cut the cake. Did you?"

Becca shook her head. "I don't know where she got off to.

I asked those girlfriends of hers. I got the feeling the one — what's her name, Suzie? — was a little stoned. I couldn't get a straight answer." She sighed, bending to slide her shoes from her feet. He heard her groan with pleasure. "Always the best part of any evening," she said, smiling slightly.

JT wasn't smiling. "How can you be so blasé? Maddie disappeared!"

Becca rolled her eyes. "Sweetheart, I think you're being a little dramatic. She might have run off to one of the guest houses, or to one of her friend's houses. Who knows? I wouldn't be so certain she's missing. She'll show up in the morning — probably hungover."

They walked upstairs side-by-side. "This doesn't feel right," JT said. "I hate the idea of going to bed without knowing where she is."

Becca sighed. "Would it make you feel better to ride around looking for her? I'll go with you, if you want."

He pulled off his bow tie, unbuttoning his shirt. "I don't

know. As much as I want to drag her back to the house by her hair, I know you're right. She'll show up in the morning or sneak back in overnight like nothing happened."

"She's eighteen, honey. She can do as she pleases." He followed Becca to her room, where she removed her earrings and the necklace he'd given her that evening. She ran her fingertips over it and smiled in the mirror. "This is so beautiful," she murmured, smiling at his reflection over her shoulder.

"*You're* so beautiful. I'm always proud to show you off." His hands ran down her arms as his mouth grazed the back of her neck. It had been a long time since they'd been together.

"Oh, sweetie." She sighed, and JT had heard that sigh before. The moment was over.

"No?"

"I'm exhausted." She turned to him, planting a light his on the corner of his mouth. "It's been a long day—a long week, really."

He shrugged. It was typical. He turned to leave the room. "Goodnight, then."

"Hang on a second, please." The tone of her voice had changed. She was no longer sweet, adoring Becca. This was the tough-as-nails Becca he was accustomed to.

"Yes?" He turned, smiling.

"Don't give me that sweet smile, Mr. Rossi." She slid the dress from her shoulder, letting it fall to the floor. He stirred below the waist. Did she know how she drove him crazy? He would have bet on it.

"What is it, then?" He forced himself to look her in the eye rather than focusing on her perfect body. No one would know she'd given birth to two children or that she was over forty.

She slid into a dressing gown, then sat at her vanity to take the pins from her hair. Her eyes never left his in the mirror. "What was that deal Stephen was talking about at the party?"

He should have known she would bring that up. His wife didn't miss a thing. Stephen was no more discreet than he'd been when they were young. It was amazing that he managed to stay in office; he was such a big mouth.

"I thought you were exhausted," he pointed out, crossing his arms.

ABOUT THE AUTHOR

Toni House is an entrepreneur, novelist and mother. She began writing and reading stories at an early age, but as time went on, she put her writing on hold until 2009 when she published her first nonfiction self-help book. Her second nonfiction self-help book was published in 2010. Her true love is writing and telling stories that readers will love.

Her first fiction novel, **Song of The Red Wolf**, is based loosely on true events. It is the first in a three-book series, **The Tala Chronicles**. Published Sept. 2015.

The story starts off in Decatur Alabama then moves to a fictional town of Mystery Acres just across the bridge of the Alabama River from Camden Alabama.

The second book in **The Tala Chronicles is "1675 Deer Run Ridge"** the address of the house in each of the three books. Mystery Acres, Alabama. It will be out Summer 2016

Book 3 in *The Tala Chronicles, Red Moon Rising* will be out Spring 2017

She also plans to publish a spinoff novel, *Winter Snow,* out Summer 2017 about a Native American princess.

Senses Beyond, Book 1 *The Tala Chronicles* mini-series. Published in Jan. 2016.

Book 2 in *The Tala Chronicles mini-series, Before Tomorrow* out late Summer 2016.

Gathering Storm. Out April 2016 is the first book in Toni's new 10 book series *The Halcyon Saga.* Book 2 in *The Halcyon Saga, Web Of Lies*. Out May 2016.

A series you are sure to love. If you like the 90's TV show "Dallas" or the TV show "Scandal" or "Blood and Oil" you will love Toni's new series.

Butterfly Wings. Book 1 *The Tuscumbia Cove Series.* Toni's 4th series takes place in the small town of Tuscumbia, Alabama.

Toni was born and raised in Alabama and Toni lived in the

western United States for many years and now she resides in Decatur Alabama with her family and two of the sweetest fur babies on the planet.

Contact: Toni House www.tonihouseauthor.com

Marketingsourcebooks@gmail.com

ToniHouseAuthor@gmail.com